STREETS OF TACOMA

by Billy

Cover design and computer image: Ron Lloyd
Back cover photo: Rick Moller
Editor and Pre-Press Production: Chris Thomsen

Songs:
"Again" by Newman & Cochran
"It Can't Be Wrong" by Steiner & Gannon
"Once" by Russell & Spina, Copyright © 1951 Hub Music assigned 1969 Harrison Music Corporation/Spina Music, renewed 1979, International copyright secured

Printed by Thomson-Shore, Inc.
7300 West Joy Road
Dexter, Michigan 48130-9701

To Moon

Acknowledgements

Thanks to the wonderful
Barney, Chad, Connie, Dave, Dawn, Dick, Jeff,
Jim, Jock, Joe, Larry, Shirley and Zack
for their encouragement.

Special thanks to
Brenda Lee Davidson, Marjorie Hanson,
Nicole Hanson, Sarah Heldman,
Ron Lloyd and Jim Wilke
for their assistance and guidance.

Dear Reader,

I've spent thirty years playing around with this little tale. In spite of my time, it's meant to take little of yours, more like a drama than a lengthy novel–a fast read of two or three sittings, perhaps five hours in all. I call it a *quick novel*; see if you agree.

Prologue

It began as a dream in soft sunshine. And so, the soft westerly coming down the Strait of Juan de Fuca joined with an equally soft northerly at Admiralty Inlet turning south into Puget Sound. It lifted the tender willows and ignored the stiffer alders as it left Marrowstone to starboard, slipped into Mutiny Bay to port rejecting its bluff, angled back to Point No Point to starboard, slightly gaining speed with the waning flood, whooshed past Kingston, Shilshole and Seattle, bucking the first of the ebb as it accelerated through the venturi between Blake and Vashon Islands, scampering along the thirteen mile stretch down Colvos Passage to Point Defiance, compressing as it cleared the giant smelter stack, moving east along the bluff past Ruston through north Tacoma, now in a huff as if annoyed by the spires of Stadium High School and then turning more southerly down Saint Helens Avenue (yet a river all the same), and there falling upon a white sloop sailed by four struggling upwind to hoist, first the main, then the jib. The little ship harnesses the feisty wind and then surfs downwind past the House of Moon to starboard, then the Temple Theater to port. The shorter of the two men at the helm struggles to keep the boat under the sails. They shoot past the *News Tribune* towards the confluence of Saint Helens, Broadway and Ninth Street with its island midstream. The torrent, as if from falls, sweeps down Ninth to meet the run from Saint Helens. It is here they will be tested. They had previously conquered the violent coupling at fifteen knots, then twenty, but could they handle thirty? At twenty there were only turbulent rollers but now there were violent breakers, could they? Here is the confluence, now! They surf down the first breaker, all scream for joy as the knot-meter sweeps past twelve. The second breaker hits them abeam but the helmsman holds, and the boat comes back under the sails. They scream again as they see fourteen on the meter. But the third breaker catches the stern and sweeps it violently to port. The boom attempts to jibe, but the preventer stops it, and they are pinned! The helmsman corrects but the yacht doesn't answer the helm and a fourth breaker lifts them. The boat is temporarily airborne above the island. Then it crashes in the torrent's fit of rage. The mast breaks at the spreaders, the hull splits amidships, and the deck is awash. A dark, young woman floats across the bow, first lodged at the stem as a voluptuous figurehead, then floating away–lost. The taller of the young men staggers after her but a breaker engulfs him and he, too, is lost.

The second woman clings to the mast, as a heinous monster leaps aboard and advances toward her. The helmsman struggles to intercept it, but the intruder knocks him aside. He grabs the monster's leg and they are both washed overboard, but the agile helmsman reaches back, clutches a lifeline as the enemy is carried away by the breaker. The helmsman and woman embrace, then slide down the broken portion of the mast on the leeward side of the hull and escape.

Moon

Hi, this is Moon. I'm standing right now on the corner of Ninth and Broadway, or you could call it Ninth and St. Helens if you wanted. It's not so much a corner as a square, rather like Times Square. I've never been to Times Square but I've seen pictures of a tall, pointed building centering a broad fairway; and that's what we have here, a tall triangular shaped building that divides St. Helens and Broadway into a "Y." This is a grand square for a town the size of Tacoma.

My back is to the Music Box Theater, appropriately named because there's something magic about its Gothic architecture that trips your fantasies. Below it is Don's Cafe, a hip place to hang. In fact, this entire square is the hangout for nightlife in the city. To my right a half block is the Beverly Theater, across the alley from the Music Box is the Rialto, and directly across the four lanes with its pedestrian island in the center is the Roxy Theater. The Winthrop Hotel, Tacoma's finest, is kitty-corner from me on the northeast. There are at least ten restaurants within a block. The remaining establishments are fine clothing, gift, and jewelry stores. I can stand here by the hour because sooner or later everyone I know or want to know will come by.

And the chicks, they get dressed in their finery and parade here. I can fall in love a dozen times each night. Then for humor, there's *The Riders of the Purple Sage*. That's what we call the cowboys. They ride their mounts–these machines, chair cars, hot rods or plain old jalopies, round and round the block. The rider's window will be rolled down rain or shine, his biceps will be flattened against the window frame to make it appear larger. If they come too close, I'll smell stale beer and chips. If I can hold my disgust, they're good for a laugh. But what the hell, they're probably laughing at me and that's okay because I'm standing here in the drizzle, water is running down my duck's ass hairdo, my suedes are soaked, it's 46 degrees, but I'm cool. I get to tell you this story:

> Hey, Tacoma,
> Your winter solstice is near,
> The darkest meridian is here.
> Slither you serpent, scoot, scatter.
> Ah, Moon, how your mouth doth chatter!

Haaaaw!

I've always been a storyteller. I've never really written anything, but cats would gather around and I could keep them as long as I wanted. I'd be telling them about Kid, Whitey, Babs, Abby and the time Kid took us to the boat house at Point Defiance Park and turned it into a midnight dance pavilion. That brought every fuzz in town. There were close to 200 cats with nary an arrest. Before I'd even finish the telling, they'd call out, "Write it down, Moon, put it on paper." I've got to admit I've tried a time or two but it wouldn't start out right. I think it was because I lacked the feel of Tacoma, the real Tacoma, because these things couldn't happen anywhere else. This time I've got help–Kid and Stella, besides I've quit the sauce. Hey wait, I'm getting ahead of myself.

Let me make some introductions. You'll be meeting the Kid, his real name is Curtis Dahl, but Star is the only one I ever heard call him that. He'll be doing most of the early writing because he knows the streets of Tacoma like no one else. You pay attention and believe what he says–he is the only one I've ever known who is incapable of lying. I'll come in during the teen years, then Stella plans to gather things up in for the denouement (she loves that word). Stella's sort of an observer/participant; that's what they'd call her in one of Kid's fancy lit classes. But don't get the idea this is going to be literature; put this book down right now if that's what you want because this ain't it!

Kid

My name is Curtis Dahl, though they call me Kid, the Kid. At this point, it's embarrassing but there's nothing I can or want to do about it. But more about that later.

I've read what Moon said about himself in his opening remarks. I'd just say, reserve judgement on him. There's a chunk of humanity there, if for no other reason than he can laugh. His face will open to a thousand wrinkles, tears will flow, he'll stumble and perhaps even fall. He'll bring everyone near to uncontrolled laughter. Man, he can laugh. And then there's his horn–his wild and wicked sax. Corky Corcoran's dad was in the audience one night when Moon was doing his raunchy "Stormy Weather." "The world waits for this one," he whispered.

I guess you already know Moon asked me to write this. He thinks it's a story that requires telling. I'm not so sure that isn't just his ego talking. But I owe him, besides who can argue with the great Moon, so here goes.

He picked a reasonable candidate because it's easy for me to remember. I can crawl into the past through the smell of Lincoln cordovan shoe polish, the taste of Nel's green onion burgers, the pain of sweat running into the cut on my puffed lip, the touch of my face chasing the scent of Shocking perfume across her cheek, her ear. I remember the bell going off and I'm in my corner blowing spit-water in the air in my silly way. I can put on a Kenton recording and sit back and hear that piano. I can see Stan's strong, blond fingers driving those keys. I watch that horn section stand–pushing, pushing, then the sax solo stings, catches me, my breath comes hard as the piano picks it up again; and I'm back on the streets of Tacoma. The jazz is "Artistry Jumps" and I'm a kid again and promising always to be the Kid.

Wait; let me bring some chronology to this. I was born in University Place, west of the city and moved to my grandmother's house on 1805 South "L" Street when I started the first grade in 1940. My best friend was Yosi Yako. His family owned the corner grocery on 19th and K Street. He was generous with his toys and treats from the store. He didn't know how to say "mine." We walked seven blocks to Stanley School every morning. One day when we were in the second grade, we cut through Mrs. Musso's garden patch. Yosi pulled some garlic, he loved the stuff so I ate some too. An hour later the principal walked right into Miss Ring's classroom and marched Yosi and me to the office. I guess we hadn't realized the power of fresh garlic, and we hadn't noticed Mrs. Musso watching us through her upstairs window. It was no big deal; the nurse gave us a tooth brushing and sent us back to class. When I went by to get Yosi before school the next day, Yosi said he couldn't go.

"Why, Yosi?" I said, "Miss Ring wants you, come on!" I pulled his arm. His mother bent down and kissed us. I didn't know why she was crying.

"You go with Curtis, Yosi. I'll come and get you later," she said. It was right after Spelling. I had missed two, so I was at the blackboard. The principal walked in again; someone was in the hall in a uniform. Yosi was being marched out, alone. He tried to look tough but Yosi was never tough.

His frightened eyes caught mine as he neared the door. I stopped Miss Ring asking if I could go with him. "No," she said, "There's no place for *your* kind there." Arlene Mininger started crying. I wished she hadn't because I started to sniffle. "This war will be over soon," Miss Ring continued, "The internment camps aren't so bad."

I wondered what *kind* I was? I knew, we all knew, what kind Yosi was. He was good. I decided I'd have to work on being good to be Yosi's kind.

I know Yosi had never gone to Sunday school, but I had to–like it or not. My mother wet my cowlick, ran a comb through it, and pushed me and a half dozen other siblings out the door. My big brothers didn't have to go. "Don't stop at that old Catholic Church," my mother would call after us. She was frightened of the *Papist* as she called them. Her grandparents had been wealthy Protestants from Sian Mills near Limerick and you could almost hear the chant run through the family: *The Catholics are coming, the Catholics are coming!* But I'd always stop there anyway on my way to Beth Lutheran. The Catholics would give you a Milky Way or a Mars Bar. All the old Lutherans offered were jellybeans and then only two or three. During the Christmas recital, I did "Little Boy Blue." They gave me a little blue bugle, which they insisted I take home for practice. I didn't need much practice. The piece asked that I blow it once softly at the beginning and then twice terribly hard at the ending. There was a large crowd at the performance. I got a big applause and much laughter. Everyone, even the minister, gave me a pat on the back. Then they made me give the bugle back. I had thought it was mine. It couldn't have cost a quarter, heck, a dime. It wasn't that I was so fond of that dumb horn, but

Yosi liked it. I was going to give it to him. He'd given me so much.

After Yosi was taken to the concentration camp, in fact the very next Sunday, I told my Sunday school teacher, Miss Lindquist, I didn't believe in God. She quietly ushered me out of the class and she held me while she called the minister. What did she think? I was going to run away?

"How old are you, son?" the minister asked.

"I'm seven," I said.

"Now, at seven, you say there is no God. You know this much?"

"No," I answered, "I didn't say there was no God. What I did say was that I don't believe in Him. He's not nice. He is supposed to be so all-powerful and He lets them take Yosi Yako to the concentration camp. Yosi is good. God should have known that. He didn't help. He's not good like Yosi. I hate Him."

The following Sunday, instead of Sunday school, I followed my big brothers downtown to sell papers. I had a nickel so we stopped at a pop stand and I bought a Pepsi Cola. We all took swigs. Some went up my nose, because I was reading their slogan: "Ten full ounces that's a lot, for a nickel, too. Pepsi Cola is the drink for you!" I recited it all the way down to the *Tacoma Times*. "Twelve full ounces that's a lot, twice as much for a nickel, too, Pepsi Cola's the drink for you!"

My father finally got a real job, we left my grandmother's house and moved to a semi-rural area ten miles southeast of town. My dad was a bright man. He could build a radio, a piano, or a tractor from scratch. But he could never work for another man, so that *real* job didn't last long either. Our family knew only hunger and want. A Mrs. Vale and some nice charity women would bring a few goodies by for Thanksgiving and Christmas. They'd smile like they'd just given the Keys to the Kingdom. What did they think we did the rest of the year? I wanted to throw them out but my mother needed them.

Our house was mostly built of shiplap with tarpaper to keep out the wind and rain. There was some white Armstrong siding across a major portion of the front. Our five-acre plot was wonderful though. It had, some eons ago, been a small lake but plant succession had reclaimed it. Still little springs would sprout up here and there as the water table rose. The small knoll in front of the house supported a huge triple-trunked maple that gave shade and provided structure for a tire swing and a pair of steel hoops.

A small group of alders was making its presence felt among some vine maples in the back yard. The maples made for fine swinging and the alders made for fine switching. As my dad's emotions rose, he's stroll out back and cut a dozen switches. It might take him a half-hour, it was a painstaking assignment. By God, we could just wait; it would be done properly. He'd start whipping my oldest brother. He was usually the one who had committed the infraction. My mother would attempt to intercede when he really got crazy but she was little and powerless and usually got a few stings for her effort. He was usually tiring by the time he got to me, but I'd still have cuts where the angry alders dug into me.

There didn't prove to be much money in selling papers, so I started shining shoes. I figured as long as Fort Lewis was there with its 50,000 troops, I could do some business. Most of my cash I gave freely to my mother. It wasn't nearly enough to feed the family but it helped. Mom was grateful and that felt good. Sometimes I held out a little but that made me uncomfortable. I liked what I was doing, I loved the streets, and I had freedom from supervision. I'd catch the bus right after school and be downtown by four o'clock and catch the nine-thirty bus home. On weekends, they had an eleven o'clock bus and sometimes I'd catch that one. My shine kit was my ticket, when a cop saw a kid with a shine box, he knew what the kid was about so he didn't hassle him.

I'd get off the bus at 13th and Pacific Avenue and start my rounds. That was where the military buses from Fort Lewis and McChord Field unloaded. (There was also a Navy base out on the tide flats but it was much smaller.) This was the corner of my world. There was Phil Brodsky's Army-Navy Store on the northeast corner, Bennie's Clothing on the northwest, Seamore's Army-Navy Surplus on the southwest and derelict buildings on the other corner. Downstairs under Brodsky's was the USO. I'd hit that first and check for servicemen. "Want a shine, soldier?" I'd ask.

"How much?" he'd ask.

Asking that, I knew I had him, his fifteen cents was in my jeans. But if he said, "No," my reply was, "Bet, if I can tell you the state you were born in, you'd get a shine?"

"Sure!" he'd say.

"You were born in the state of infancy!" I'd quickly answer.

We'd all laugh. "Guess you got me, kid!"

There were risks, too. Sometimes someone would want you to come to his room and shine the extra shoes he had there. Elders always told me never to do it but I wasn't afraid and people seemed to know it. If someone started something with me, I had plans of my own to protect myself. I'd go up there if I was guaranteed at least three pairs. I never did get in trouble, myself. One time a crazy guy picked Donny Murdock up by his scrotum and his left arm. I put my shoebox up the side of his head. He was all bloody but he shouldn't have done that.

If there were nothing at that USO, I'd walk the four blocks up the hill to the big USO on Fawcett Avenue. They had jukebox dancing there almost every afternoon. I'd do better if there was no dancing. The soldiers looked homesick, and I think they'd get a shine just for a diversion. When there was dancing, I'd always stay and watch awhile. I learned a lot just watching. I'd see these bus loads of girls from neighboring small towns like Puyallup, Sumner, Buckley and Roy, unloading delicate, young girls. Rules were they had to stay in the building until they left for home on the bus. There were lots of chaperones, so it was safe. The Mothers for the War Effort made certain of that!

Kid

By the time I was 11, I wanted to learn how to jitterbug. At the USO, you could watch some really competent East Coast dancers. This corporal, maybe 22, was cool. He was teaching this shy, but beautiful girl, maybe 17, how to 'bug. He'd slow-time swing her, flip her and dip her. Then he'd speed up. She started getting into it. She'd laugh and then put her hand over her mouth, not risking too much. Next, Nat King Cole on the jukebox was asking us to believe in the "Paper Moon." You'd see the corporal in half-time now, gently rocking her, his right thigh pressing her crotch–her perineum, as my sister's anatomy book called it–and she'd be just staring in space, as her body was betraying her. Twenty-five Sumner mothers sitting in the little, hard folding chairs, watching–but seeing nothing. After all, they'd done their part. I'd heard them talking. They'd brought three buses while the much larger Puyallup only brought two. As Nat Cole signed off, the dancer deftly pulled his girl through the crowd and was first to the big red, white and blue nickelodeon where he pushed D-23. The big arm that had just shelved "Paper Moon" now brought out "Wrong." And, the couple snuggled together as Billy Ekstine's deep voice, perhaps the sexiest voice of the century, reached back in the bass ranges and sang:

Wrong, would it be wrong to kiss?
Seeing I feel like this?

Would it be wrong to try?
Wrong, would it be wrong to stay here
In your arms this way, under this starry sky?
If it is wrong, why were you sent to me?
Why am I content to be with you forever?
So when I need you so much and I have waited
        so long
It must be right, it can't be wrong.

A tender sax solo follows, then a repeat of the chorus. The song ends having made its contribution to the war effort. The couple looks like they are about to kiss. Their lips move close. This, the chaperones do notice and look uneasy for a moment. But then the corporal steps backwards and shakes her hand; slips his cap from of his rear pocket, steps forward again, whispers in her ear, waves goodbye and leaves by the only apparent exit. She walks to the rear and enters the ladies room. My curiosity made me stay through several sets, but she never came out. After, I walked around the Fawcett side of the building. Sure enough, there was the window, half-open. Up the hill a block was the *ask no questions* Griffin Hotel. I bet he never even had to tell her he was going overseas. Darn, I wanted to learn how to dance!

By that time, I'd been on the street for almost five years. I know I was into things that were not the norm. I watched lots of movies. I should be saying, "Awe, gee, shucks," that's what kids said in the movies. Then, too, I'd always liked girls. Arlene Mininger was my first girlfriend (though she never knew it). I'd never in my life said, "Girls, yuck!" Boys, we were told, were "Rats and snails and puppy dog tails," but girls were "Sugar and spice and everything nice." I never doubted that. I had the idea that it took a girl to complete me. I couldn't imagine it another way. Like in the movies I could see myself with a silk ascot kissing the hand of a rare delicacy. So, I'd watch men with women, weighing, judging every move. I saw myself as an observer waiting for my chance to participate. And I knew I'd be okay when it did come. I had an image of myself as ahead of the game. I had a little to spare. I wouldn't let myself get out of control. It was easy for me to be fair. I knew that corporal wasn't fair. He was too experienced for that young girl. He was catching trout in a fish farm. I wasn't outraged though. It's just the things men and women did together–what could you say? Life wasn't always fair but I knew I could be.

　　　　Everyone in our family was smart as far as IQ went. My older sister skipped two grades. My oldest brother was very smart but he was never fair; he was not good. My second brother was better but still not good enough. My sisters were very good, but not so good as Yosi. It was better, I saw, to pick your friends outside your family–that way you had control. If you lost control, only injury and shame could follow. I'd see a drunk get into an argument with a policeman, next three cops would be dragging his unconscious body into a paddy wagon. I'd see a shipyard worker put his whole paycheck into the pinball machines and not even have bus fare. Worse, I'd see a good man like Charley Gross fall. He was a middle-aged guy, hard working. He owned the taxi and cigar counter in front of the Tivoli. At that start of the War, he had one cab, now in 1945 he had eight. His cabs, always spiffy, were white with a blue top; naturally they were called Blue Top Taxis. Charley kept himself spiffy, too; he'd get a shine every other day. His wife, I have to admit, was a looker. She'd help dispatch and run the cigar counter. The war bucks rolled in, more money than they had experience to deal with. Charley was always swell to me, he'd always want to take me to lunch at the Husk Cafe in exchange for the shine. My BLT with shake cost him fifty cents, a lot more than his fifteen cent shine. It embarrassed me to take such an advantage, but there was no way to say no to Charley. After a while, I started noticing whiskey on his breath. His wife started making long trips to the beauty parlor; clever hairdos and fancy clothes. One day Charley fired a driver for being a few minutes late–so unlike him. Another time his wife cussed out a customer. He looked so humble as he staggered away. "There's just so much I can take from his kind–big buck nigger."

"His kind," I said, "I'm his kind." She started to turn into me but stopped. I never saw her again. Rumor was she left with a flyer from McChord Field, ten years her junior. Charley drove his car into a bridge near Roy, killing a young female companion. Charley lost everything, including his right foot.

After I worked the big USO, I'd walk across the street and down a half block to Nel's Burgers with "the works." Nel's old man, Herb, was the master, he'd pile on the goodies so your mouth would scarcely fit. You'd find yourself chasing the patty as it skittered about. You'd have to stand and lean forward, otherwise the drippings would wipe out your clothing. Half a block away you'd notice a blob on your shirt anyway.

My next stop would be the Negro district on lower Broadway. Actually, 13th was the dividing line. Everything south was lower whether it was Broadway or Pacific. Colored people called me "Little Whitey." "Little Whitey, you're the best little boot white in town," or "Little Whitey, you can give me a shine but don't you call me Shine." There was always a lot of laughing. About mid-block was a major cabaret; that would be my destination. I walked right in. They didn't seem to care about the Minor Law. "Little Whitey's a business man, he can go anywhere he wants."

Sometimes I'd go behind to the whorehouse, but only if Cadillac Jonesy took me. He seemed to control the access. It was real special for me. The piano player would be picking away at the keys. The girls would bring out all manner of shoes–red, gold, rhinestone. Most I couldn't shine but there were some leathers and a few alligators I could do. They made me feel welcome. I'd sit in the middle of the floor and they'd circle telling how they wanted their shoes done and asking questions about my family and school. They weren't just asking like most adults did. You could tell they were interested in the answers. They gave me a hug for almost no reason. There was this young blond, perhaps sixteen or seventeen. She was especially attentive to me. Amanda, she was the madam, I called her Queen. One day Queen led me into her room to help her put her shoes away, she said. She closed the door behind us. I had a crush on her. I began to get all jittery. She put her arms around me, hugging me and crying. "I've a little brother just like you," she cried, "I'll never see him again." I pulled away, feeling a fool.

Pacific Avenue south of 13th was my money making district. Seymour's Army-Navy Surplus was on the southwest corner. The Salvation Army band played there every night. I liked their noise. Soldiers caught the buses back to Fort Lewis there, so I could count on a couple of shines. Next door was a pawnshop, next to that was the popular 1306, a large cabaret. I couldn't get in there but I could sneak into lots of the regular taverns. The next four blocks held little else but taverns, restaurants, pawnshops and cheap hotels. There were two *redemption* centers. The bible thumpers worked this area pretty hard. Also, there was one clothing store, one poolroom, one shoeshine parlor and the one and only Shell Theater. The Shell showed kids' cowboy shows. You could watch Roy Rogers beat up some outlaw, while some well-dressed man would sit next to you and throw his raincoat over both your laps and his fingers would come a-walking. I'd shove him away; if he did it again I'd leave. Out front was Dooley's Shine Parlor. When Dooley would see me coming, he'd say, "What's shakin', Little Whitey?"

I'd answer, "There ain't nothing shakin' but the peas in the pot."

"And they wouldn't be shakin' if the water wasn't hot," he'd come back.

Then it would be my turn. "What's shakin', Bra?"

"There ain't nothing shakin' but the leaves on the trees," he'd say.

"And they wouldn't be shakin' if it wasn't for the breeze," I'd come back. Then we'd do a thumb and pinky handshake and everyone would laugh.

Two doors down was Bert's Good Eats. I could often get a couple of customers there. Besides, they had great cantaloupe, a full half for a dime and for a nickel, they'd put two scoops of vanilla in the center. The Anchor was my favorite tavern. The sailors hung out there. It had these old-fashioned saloon doors like in cowboy shows. I could sneak right underneath. A sailor would stick out his foot, and I'd have his money before the bartender caught wise. The sailors were more fun than the soldiers—more crazy. Woody Herman was their band. They could get there with Hampton, too. They'd be singing, "Hey, hey, hey, babba reebah. Mama's on the couch, papa's on the top, baby's on the floor, shouting, shoot it to her pop!"

I loved those guys. They'd all been to war in the South Pacific. They all had a chest full of ribbons; and they'd all be going back soon. But, by God, Uncle Sam was going to get a worn and weary carcass when their ship sailed. Maybe I was prejudiced in their favor because they were tippers. One in five soldiers tipped, all the sailors did.

The B&M Tavern was my nemesis. The big, red-headed bartender would grab my arm holding my shine box, spilling rags and brushes; and cans of Shinola and Lincoln would be rolling all over the place. The rest of the people were nice, however; I'd wait outside and the barmaid and customers would bring everything to me. I had a lot of friends on that street. Even when they wouldn't let me come in, they'd bring their shoes out to me; often barefooted.

The Union Station represented the south end of my route, beyond that was strictly industrial. The station wasn't much in the way of a money maker for me but I loved to look at it with its great copper dome, tarnished all green and beautiful. You walked through this mammoth, vaulted entrance into an all-marble interior. It gave you the feeling of being in ancient Greece. Stranded wartime travelers would be sleeping in these huge oak benches. If you had to sleep in public the Union Station was the classiest bed you could aspire to. To me there were only three notable large structures in town: the Medical Arts Building, the Rust Building and the Union Station. The others rated two and three while the Station was a perfect ten. Oh yeah, the City Hall was cool, too.

After the Station, I'd walk up the east side of Pacific. It was a fast walk because there wasn't much there. On the triangular corner of 17th, there was the airline ticket office, then a bunch of beat-up vacant storefronts, a pretty nice restaurant, a vacancy or two and then the unemployment office. All pretty boring stuff. On the corner of 15th was Schoenfeld's Furniture, a half century-old store that had been passed by as the city moved north. The Greyhound Bus Depot was on the corner of 14th, and between 14th and 13th was absolutely nothing but old, deserted buildings with dates like 1888 on their fronts. From 13th to 12th was an area I liked. The USO and Brodsky's, as I mentioned before, were on the corner, next a sporting goods store; then the Husk Cafe and a hotel, I can't think of the name, where scantily dressed ladies would hang out the window; then a nondescript tavern, and finally, the Tivoli Tavern & Card Room. The Tivoli was sort of a home base for me. Its entrance was set back from the street which left room for a cigar stand and taxi dispatch and the entrance to first, a penny arcade downstairs, and later, Jack's Pool Hall with my shoeshine stand on the landing. Lots of old Scandinavians hung out at the Tiv. They saw my hair and features and took me to be one of theirs. Many of them had come from the Old Country in their late twenties and early thirties with too much foreign accent to interest young American girls. Thus, they stayed single. They'd put in their eight hours at the mill or cabinet shop, change clothes and would be at the Tivoli by five p.m., buy a tin of Copenhagen at the cigar counter, tap it twice with their index finger, press a wad under the lip and have their shoes shined. They asked me about my life but told me very little about theirs. (Well, there was Old Al; he was always bragging about his widow friend.) Mostly, they gave me advice. I knew they cared about me because if I didn't show up for a couple of days, they'd be right out there when I returned, seeing what was up.

When I left the Tivoli, I'd always cross to the west side of the street and backtrack to 13th. Bennie's was there on the corner. It had wild and wonderful clothes. I'd see myself in them and dream. Then I'd go around the corner to the Dixie Dairy ice cream parlor. They gave you two scoops for a nickel and sometimes three. It was the local hangout for a fun-loving late teenage set. The banter never quit and often I could join in. I guess I was kind of accepted. After the Dairy, I'd go back past Bennie's, Jenning's Hardware, the Safeway, and then past four other clothing stores. The Cameo Theater was mid-block and pretty much like the Shell but in a little better condition, so it cost a dime more. The Club Smoke Shop was next. All the merchant restaurants that put on airs were called smoke shops. They'd sell pipes, tobacco and their lunches were usually a little upscale. But what they all had in common were smart looking, sharp talking, dice throwing women. The Club was no exception. They played 4-5-6 for money or the check. No self-respecting clothing store owner could just pay his lunch check, he had to roll double or nothing. The Club had a beautiful window—two giant rotisseries, one pork, one beef, with juices always dripping; highlighted by amber and red heat lamps that made them look like feasts for the gods. The Club had Jackie, also a feast. About 5'9", but easily 6' with heels. She had full breasts and a pinched waist with full hips. Her necklines plunged almost to her waist. She also had a full head of red hair, piled high on her head and she had huge, green eyes, which teased one and all!

One day Bennie, who seemed to like everyone, including me, saw me looking in his window. "Come on, boy," he said, "I'm going to the Club for hot beef and I need someone to talk at." He had my arm and we were off. As we were finishing our roast beef, he mentioned that he had to hurry to meet his wife for some shopping. He didn't look happy. He approached Jackie with the check, obviously in a hurry.

Jackie said, "Bennie, what's that face all about, when you come to see your Jackie?" She puts both palms on the counter and leans her cleavage towards him. Bennie is stopped. "Bessie being a little stingy with that *good* stuff?" she asked in a stage whisper. She picked up the dice, dropped them in the leather bucket, and began to shake them vigorously. Her bosoms bouncing teasingly, "And now you've come to take all poor Jackie's got!"

"Cut the crap," Bennie says, "Roll 'em."

After the Club, I remained on the west side of the street because the east side had mostly commercial stuff: the National Bank of Washington, Puget Sound National Bank and a few nondescript shops, then the People's Department Store on the corner of 11th. But my side had three menswear stores, three restaurants, a shoe repair shop, a cabaret, a savings and loan, and the famous Long John Silver. He was one-legged–a silent screen star, he told everyone. He looked like Silver; he talked like Silver and that was good enough for me–he was Silver. He sold papers on the corner of 11th Street. When I'd come by, he'd say, "How's it hangin', Boy?"

I'd say something like, "About a foot lower than yours, dragging right on the old ground" or if it was raining, I'd say "Gee, this water is cold."

And he'd holler with his big, booming voice, "Sneeze, little one, your bean is dusty!" or "Keep on spouting, you're a whale!"

Eleventh Street was the center of town and by far the busiest. It had the Post Office on "A" Street, People's on Pacific Avenue, Manning's Market & Cafeteria on Commerce and Fishers and Rhodes Brothers department stores on Broadway. I crossed 11th and passed the Rust Building with its big men's store. Mid-block was Murphy's, a great restaurant that served delicious, tiny oysters as small as the tip of your little finger. There wasn't too much more on the block for me–Washington Hardware and one more tavern I couldn't go in, and then the Reviera Theater–several steps up from the Cameo and Shell but still showing kids' movies as well as older adult stuff. On the corner was the City Cigar Store. It was *the* place as far as tobacco shops went. There was another cigar store on the east side of the street that had a great wooden Indian. It also had pictures of Tacoma from 1909 when the owner was a boy. He could point to every storefront and tell me exactly what was there when he was my age. He told me in his day the Reviera had been for those vaudeville performers who were not good enough to play at the Pantages. The Pantages was the former burlesque house we now called the Roxy Theater.

The northern end of my route was the Turf Smoke Shop. It was just off Ninth and Commerce and was the best place in town for an 11-year-old boy. First, it had horse racing in the back room, cards in the middle section, a restaurant in the front area and Gilda at the dice counter. There were so many laws broken in that place every minute that they didn't bother with me. I had the run of the shop. There were also lots of high rollers. I could count on a half dozen shines on a good day. Gilda was a little like Jackie, only more so. She was a bleached-blond with a Betty Hutton shape and personality, only naughtier. She loved to tease me. She'd call me over to the counter. I knew better than to go, but I always did. She'd talk low and sweet saying, "Hi, Sweet Pea. You got that little *stinger* of yours wet, yet?" Then she'd come up with the biggest laugh. Next, the waitresses would sneak over to see what she'd said to me. Soon the whole place would be howling. And there I was, stuck shining someone's shoes and couldn't get away.

Kid

When I was 13, I started boxing. Lots of kids did it then. I wasn't much good at throwing or catching but I could hit whether it was a bat, golf club, tennis racket or my fists. Tacoma was a fight town. There were two major boxing gyms in the city–the Police Gym, of course, run by the police, and the Starlight Athletic Club, some said, run by the mob. The apparent proprietor was a fast talkin' Italian saloonkeeper, Mr. Bianco; but the two trainers were real winners. One was an old Jewish guy named Gabe who worked with all the younger kids. "Hey, Kid", he'd say to me, "Did you cock today? Ha ha ha!" Why it was such a big deal to him if you had a good shit (I guess I should say BM), I never knew; but I knew I liked him. I don't know how good a coach he was, but he made me laugh a lot; and his training sessions were shorter than Harry Anderson's. Harry had a legendary reputation; it was said he was responsible for Freddie Steele's career. Steele had been Tacoma's only champion, a middleweight. And, he had also handled the great Frenchy Falentine–that is, until Frenchy was drafted and got messed up on that aircraft carrier explosion.

I was always anxious to spar but Gabe would say, "You little pischer! You've got to learn to walk, then dance, then I'll show you how to spar." So day after day, I'd stand in front of the big mirror, step together close. I'd put out a left jab in slow motion with each step. Finally, when I was

14, I had my first fight.

Every Saturday night, the Club would throw up a card of about ten bouts. We'd receive ten dollars, called "expense money." Most of our opponents came from the Police Gym, but some came from Lincoln High where they had a boxing program. I was carded to fight a 14-year-old colored kid from Salishan. I was pretty comfortable with him as an opponent. We'd sparred before, were reasonably equal, and had become friends. In our pre-fight exam, the doctor detected what might have been a heart murmur; so my opponent was disqualified. Just then, a tall kid from Lincoln stepped up.

"Put me in, I'll fight him." He was two years older, 5'11", he towered over me by six inches, weighed my same 125 lbs. He had a lean, snake-like build–no body fat. Gabe said to us, "You two can't fight, if for no other reason than everyone will laugh–a real Mutt and Jeff show!"

I didn't know whose decision it was, but the tall guy looked at me, "What's the matter? You chicken?" That made my decision. I was going to fight him whether it was in the ring or out in the street.

"Hey, let 'em fight!" Joe Bianco's rasping voice came from across the room. "That little Swede's tough; let's see what he's got." Gabe jumped over the dressing table. He could move when he wanted. I could hear him arguing with Bianco.

"The guy's got two years on him. I've seen him fight. He's got combinations my boy's never dreamed of. This is his first fight. Damn it, this is how kids get hurt!" Joe waved him off. He paid the rent; he made the decisions; I could see that.

Gabe, looking shaken, returned with Harry Anderson. We went straight to the dressing room. Gabe's silence was unnerving. Harry was the quiet kind of guy who would wink at me, but had hardly spoken before. He looked me in the eye for a long time before he spoke. I think he was checking out my attention span. Finally, he said, "The guy you're going to fight is a twerp. You can take him out, Kid, but there is only one way–my way. I'll be in your corner, I give you every move, listen now." He dropped to one knee, his eyes still holding me. "That Mick Mullens up at Lincoln teaches them how to hook, an unorthodox hook, but effective, especially if the opponent doesn't now how to handle it." He repeatedly demonstrated the hook. "Since it comes slightly overhand, it's more effective against taller guys. You're what, 5'5"? Well, I want you in a crouch. You be 3'5" when you're in there. He'll have to throw down on you. That will leave him in an awkward stance. He's good enough, he can do it, but you keep working to your right. He'll throw that hook over your head and you drop even lower and drive your right into his lower midsection. Don't even think about going to his head; the first time I see you reaching for his head, I'm throwing in the towel–it's over!" He snapped me hard with the towel he was holding. "You got that?" I nodded.

I can't really say what happened the first round. The crowd was definitely on my side. If he caught me with anything, they would boo; if I threw even the slightest punch, they would cheer. I stayed low, as Harry demanded. But my opponent was also telling me to keep low with his left jab that repeatedly stung me. I could feel my nose grow larger and my fat lips coming up to meet it. I knew I was losing. As I walked back to the corner at the end of the second round, I watched this beautiful, young woman who had been cheering for me put her hands over her face.

Harry, to my surprise, was elated. "I tell you, Kid, you're doing great! You're the best listener I've ever worked with. You keep it up. If this fight is lost; it's Harry's loss, not yours. Look, he's faster a hand and you're faster a foot. I keep seeing that little side step Gabe taught you. It's what's making him miss and look bad. Now, this is the last round, he's going to get anxious and my guess is soon. You continue your low stance, he'll throw that big one right over your left shoulder. This time, don't side step, hold your position and lift that dandy right of yours into his ribs. Got that? Not the gut anymore, I want you to raise it four inches. Got that?"

The first minute into the round, I was getting whipped. He was anxious, no doubt, but I seemed more anxious to get hit. I could feel a little cut open on my lip. I knew the ref would stop the fight if he saw it. But my opponent saw it first. I saw a faint smugness, then I saw the hook. As it went over my head, I set my foot, letting go my right hand. I was startled. His head was between my shoes. I'd heard the great *whoosh* as everyone else had. All the air went out of him and he was on the canvas writhing in pain! The ref was so shocked he ran right into me. He raised my hand on the way back to the corner and the place exploded! The woman who had put her hands over her face came up. "I love you, Kid!" she said and kissed me. I could smell whiskey on her breath as she drove her tongue down my throat. Harry laughed, pulling me away; but I could see the tears in the corner of Gabe's eyes.

"I love you, too, Kid!" he said and quietly led us through the crowd to the dressing room.

I had six more bouts that season, all easy wins. Harry never came to my corner again but Gabe took care of me, showing me little tricks that gave fun to my sport. One day I told him he was fathering me too much, getting me easy opponents. "No, Kid," he said, "Mr. Bianco personally picks all your opponents." I could see Gabe didn't much like Bianco, but I knew he liked to be around young fighters, maybe that's why he stayed. He was hard to figure.

After the second fight, they started putting "The Kid" on the fight card in place of Curtis Dahl. I didn't care. Lots of people had called me the Kid already. They said I had the kind of face that would look like a kid until I was fifty. Myself, I thought of Kid Gavilin and all the other great fighters they called Kid something-or-other.

They closed the gym the fall of '49, "just temporary," they said. I didn't much care because by that time I was also boxing at Lincoln High. It was great. I was a bit of a celebrity. In gym classes, all I had to do was box while my classmates had to do basketball and calisthenics in smelly old sweats. I was just a sophomore but I got to stroll in my satin blue and white Everlast boxing trunks and look cool. I already had a reputation for being a hard hitter. I liked that. I'd practiced on the heavy, leather bag for 20 minutes straight, intimidating the other boxers. What I was looking for was sound. The gym was a natural echo chamber. Gabe showed me how to get the maximum torque out of my right. He said those haymaker punches that John Wayne threw in the movies just shoved people around. They don't knock people out. When you hit someone, you don't want to see him tumble, because when he stops rolling, he'll get up and beat you up. What you want is torque. Your punch wants to be no longer than six inches with a lot of snap. Then, his head will end up right at your feet—he won't get up for a long time. So when I punched that big bag, I would be looking for a snap. It was fun to see how loud I could get on the bag. Lots of times the whole football team would stand around and watch. There was one sophomore, Bobby Moore; he was 6'2" and 180 lbs. He was already a star on the senior team. For some reason, he had a problem with me. He started calling me Muscles. That seemed strange to me. I was a lightweight at that time weighing about 135 lbs.; he had me by 45 lbs., so why call me Muscles? Then one day he called me Punchie. Now, that wasn't such an insult, I could have let it go; but I thought it had gone far enough. "Next time you call me Punchie, I'm going to come see what you're so proud of!" I gave him my best stare; he turned and left.

The final day of the school year, I was standing in line with my third period gym class, turning in my gear. The senior football team for some reason was sitting in the lower bleachers. Bobby was looking relaxed, leaning against the guardrail. He turned his back and said something to his teammates that I couldn't hear. Probably, "Watch this!" Then he turned to me. "Hey, Punchie!" he called. I darted towards him; he met me with a wild right, which a cow could have stepped under. I gave him a glancing right to the kidneys. He grabbed me around the shoulders. He had mile-high street shoes with leather soles; I was still wearing my boxing shoes. I spun him around and around keeping him off balance, hitting him repeatedly, first in the kidneys then in the ear. They weren't very effective punches because I could never set, but to the spectators they were points. Next, two big hands grabbed at my shoulders. I saw the football coach,

Norm Mayer, pull Bobby's arm. I was still punching when a startled Bobby Moore went on his back. I didn't knock him down–the coach pulling, Bobby ducking and those leather shoes all worked to bring him to the floor. Everyone said I put him down, even though I argued differently. I truly felt sorry for him. He was the all-star everything–a great future, but I don't know if he ever got up from that fall. He never came back to school the next year.

Once reputations are built, they aren't to be undone. Things just came my way. Things I didn't think I was asking for, but maybe I was.

There were four high schools in Tacoma, two public– Lincoln and Stadium; two Catholic _Aquinas and Bellermine. Aquinas was the girls' school; rumor had it they were fine, as we used to say then, "Fine as pure Casablanca wine in the summertime." But we poor public school cats couldn't get to them because they went to Tacoma Catholic Youth dances and it was simply impossible to get in without a TCY card. One night, Moon, my Stadium sax playing friend, said, "I've got a TCY card, let's go!" We finished off a fifth of Old Rocking Chair, which was the cheapest whiskey the state liquor stores sold. We weren't high–we were dead drunk. We slipped through the entrance. Moon fell in with this cute little Aquinas chick and I had just met the love of my night when a king-sized chaperone asked me for my TCY card. Moon, seeing the problem, charged to the rescue, falling flat on his face right between the chaperone's two big wing tips. The next thing I knew, we were surrounded by half the Bellermine football team. I was picked up over everyone by two major carriers - one under my butt and one under my shoulders. I was headed for the door. My weightlessness and intoxication made it feel like I was in flight. I could see them start to pound on Moon. I started kicking–long, heavy kicks. I don't know how, but every time my foot went out, it met a neck or a face, and they were dropping to the floor. Finally, the two guys who were carrying me realized they were assisting the battering ram and dropped me. I saw the doorknob coming towards my head, heard it hit, but felt nothing. We were on the second floor. The stairwell was mobbed–no escape! I looked back at the carnage, knew I was in real trouble if caught, saw an open window and jumped. When I stopped running to check my throbbing ankle, I was two blocks from the club. Just one problem–Moon wasn't with me. The first law of the street was if you went somewhere with someone, friend or foe, his trouble was your trouble, you didn't leave without him–drunk or not. I had to go back. I saw a cop car in front, its red lights flashing. Checking the back parking lot first, I heard a muffled sound coming from the trunk of a '46 Chev. I twisted the handle and Moon spilled out of his hiding place. We ran.

Saturday morning I took my hangover to work with me at my shine parlor on the stairwell landing between the Tivoli Tavern and Jack's Pool Hall, downstairs. The first person I saw was Harry Anderson; he always took his morning coffee at the Tiv. His eye catches my stiff ankle. Then he takes a step back like a physician doing a patient assessment. You couldn't hide these small bruises from Harry. He'd find you out but he didn't shake his head and make any judgements. Still I felt a fool. I know Harry was the untitled master of the understatement.

But, back to reputations. After the TCY scene, mine took a gigantic leap. I could feel a kind of silence when I arrived almost anyplace. Then the bravest person there would give a shy, "Hi." And then things would be almost normal, but not quite. I felt I needed to send someone ahead of me, a sentinel or something, to ease my arrival. It was eerie. Of course, I knew some of the things being said as I could always count on little Frankie Jenner to shoot off his mouth. By the time the TCY rumors were fully developed, I heard Frankie saying eleven guys were laid out–two with broken jaws, one with his eye popped out of its socket. And I'd jumped out of a three-story window–unhurt. It was bull, but what could I do? I'd already learned from the Bobby Moore scrap that denials were certain endorsements. I decided to quit going out for a while. But boredom quickly set in so I started training at the Police Gym. It was a little like going over to the enemy but with the Starlight closed, it was the only serious option and besides, Gabe and Harry were now working out of there. Gabe signed me up for the Golden Gloves Tournament. It always included the best amateur fighters from California to Canada. I had three easy bouts, then was out-pointed in the final. Everyone booed and said I was robbed, but they always say that. He was an Indian fighter from Vancouver, B.C. He had a left jab that never stopped, keeping me too unbalanced to make good use of my right. I was wishing I had Harry in my corner afterwards. I was sick and hardly civil to my friends. Three days later, when I had begun to come out of the dumps, Harry came by my shoe shine stand. "Come on, Kid, we gotta talk." Without saying another word, he led me four blocks to Firemen's Park on Ninth and A Street. I was elated because I was sure he was going to tell me he was coming back to my corner. We sat under the big totem pole, "Tallest in the World," the sign said. "This conversation is between you and me, right, Kid?" I nodded. "I've been watching you around the old Tiv for years now. I don't say much but I kind of see you like family. I mean, we're both a couple of square head Swedes, right? Maybe you've got a little Irish in you? Hey, nobody's perfect. Joe Bianca's not perfect either and he's got a lot of the devil in him. He wants me to take you back East, New Jersey, the next two summers." My heart was pounding. "He's got a brother with a string of fighters you'll train with. I'll be there to look after you." I jumped up. I was in heaven! Harry sat there–those eyes again. I sat down slowly, waiting for the other punch. "I thought you'd like it, but damn it, I don't. Bianca's willing to put thirty grand into you and he hates your kind, Kid. But you're very saleable because as he says, you're blond and pretty–that's where the money is. To him, you're just a piece of meat: put it on the table, take a few bites and push it in the gutter. I can't stand by and watch that happen."

"What's the matter, Harry, don't you think I can make it? Don't you believe in me?" I pleaded.

"Yes, I do believe in you, Kid, but as a person more than just another fighter. If you could only be a fighter, I'd say go for it. But you, you can be anything you want to be! As a fighter, sure you can make it; but for him, not for you! To be welterweight champ, that's what you want, isn't it, Kid?"

I wanted to scream, "Yes! Yes!" but again, his demeanor kept me silent.

"Look, Kid," he slowly began, "There are four abilities you must have to be champ–the ability to take a punch; the ability to dance out of trouble; and the ability to put up two good hands, a left and a right. The way I see it, you've got three out of four. You can't be champion without all four. You've got no left hand."

"I could, we could…" I began.

"It can't be taught, Kid. I can't. Gabe can't. God can't!" he continued. "Did anyone ever teach you that right hand? Hell, no! Gabe may have polished it a bit but it was there all the time. We're all given certain gifts. You were given a right that is fresh out of Tiffany's. I've never seen a better one. But without a left, you have a one-dimensional offense and worse yet, a one-dimensional defense. Sure, you can go on and win lots of fights but not the big ones. You'll take a pounding; in three years your face will look like mine. In four years, it'll shave thirty points off your IQ. To be certain, Bianca will feed you a string of bums–easy wins, maybe two years of them. He'll say, 'We're bringing the Kid along slowly.' Then he'll bring in a couple of good guys, just a little over the hill; so they'll dive. The locals will be crazy for you. Next, he'll bring in a real contender and bet the other way. He'll get his thirty grand back twenty times over."

"But look how well I've done so far," I stumbled.

"Yeah, let's look at it," he countered. "What was your best fight? I bet you're going to say your first one, aren't you?"

I nodded.

"You're right, that's the only time you've fought an older, more experienced fighter. Gabe was terrified you'd get hurt, but I knew the other guy had no right; so as long as you could circle his left, no problem. You were still getting beat–one more round and your face would have been hamburger. That killer right. What luck! *I know*, I know it was planned so you can't call it a lucky punch, but it was another kind of luck, because Ernie Jensen, the ref, told me he was just reaching for your shoulder to stop the fight when the other kid went down. Look, Kid, a fight like that with the whole world on your side can set you up for life. It can make a fool out of you, too. Consider only this: You had Gabe and me in your corner. He had no one. Now consider you with no one, and Gabe and me in *his* corner!"

I never went back to the gym–left my sweats, trunks, robe, shoes. "Give them to the needy," I told Gabe when he came by for a shine.

"Hey, Kid," he hollered on the way out, "did you cock today?"

Kid

I started spending a lot of time at the bowling alley on Ninth and Pacific. Actually, the bowling was on the third floor. I'd go to the second floor. That was as close as I ever wanted to get to bowling. The top floor was wall-to-wall alleys. The second floor, actually there was a mezzanine with a small landing between the first and second floors, so it was more like two and a half floors; anyway, we'll call it the second. The second was the lounge area, and it was huge. It had a long, long lunch counter, three pool tables, a dance floor, about a dozen large chairs and three sofas. There was an unused room that faced Pacific Avenue and there was also a quaint chapel as the place was used for the Council of Churches board meeting. Big as the place was, it had an intimacy because of the overstuffed furniture and good acoustics. I was comfortable there, most of all because the jukebox had the best jazz in town. Millie, who ran the lunch counter, was a jazz junkie who would ceremoniously smash the "Your Hit Parade" record she was replacing with something by Dexter Gordon or one of her other favorites. Also, many of the young be-bop musicians hung out there. They were wild and unpredictable, and they made me and my friends welcome. The place was officially managed by the Reverend Powers, Executive Secretary for the Council of Churches. He was an ex-collegiate wrestler and serious about his work, but he kept a loose control of the place. I liked that. I could shoot off my mouth and he'd shoot right back. It became my new headquarters. I first met Moon there; actually, he was plain old Raymond then. We'd bring records to share. He'd bring something like Gene Krupa's "Lemon Drops" and I'd bring Coleman Hawkins' "Body and Soul." Then we'd get that tall, crazy Millie who had the key to the jukebox to trade them out for a Helen O'Connell or a Frank Sinatra. It was satisfying to watch her smash that junk.

The Reverend had a temper that would just flash sometimes and when it did, he'd just say "Oops," and tuck it away. But one day, Moon enraged him. Moon had flipped him some Old Testament stuff about Moses marrying an Ethiopian. Moses' sister bitched and God sent her into the desert. "How clear of a message could He send? Huh? How clear, huh?" Moon kept it up. "Could you today marry an Ethiopian? Huh? Hell, no! You couldn't even marry a little boot chick from 15th and Broadway!" Moon riding him hard, now. "How far have we come in 3,000 years, huh? How far, huh? Huh?"

I think it was the last "huh" that did it. The Reverend grabbed Moon by the ear and was dragging him to the door. I could see serious blood coming from Moon's ear so I stepped up and popped the Reverend on the chin. He was on his butt, looking up at me ready to retaliate, then he saw Moon's ear partially torn from his jaw. He quietly thanked me and called his doctor friend.

After the Moon incident, the Reverend Powers and I became close. He knew my theology and never tried to change me. He wanted all the beautiful things for his city. A tolerance policy had existed, perhaps from Tacoma's inception. It had always been a raw, blue-collar town with its timber, its shipping, its smelting, its factories, and its military. But now, with the War behind us, the Reverend had convinced the Council of Churches, half the City Council and the Mayor, it was time for a cleansing. I knew he'd bitten into an armpit. Vice was so interlaced with the city, county, state and the mob; it was hard to tell which was which. Who were the good guys? Were there any? Some of the vice seemed necessary. There were three major whorehouses in town. How else could you service all that military? The local girls scorned them. The soldiers, once put on pedestals during WWII had now slid into the wastebasket. Indeed, if a girl even dated a serviceman, her reputation was forever tarnished. And, the tolerance system worked pretty well. Every morning you could see a dozen *working girls* waiting in line at the Health Department on Twenty-fourth and Pacific. You didn't need to be Dick Tracy to see what was going on in Tacoma. You could see Pete Petersen, the collection man, making his rounds right up front. He'd park his midnight blue Lincoln Continental in front of the Turf Smoke Shop, walk in with his Ariela Biltmore smoking away, place his empty black bank bag on Gilda's dice counter, tip his Knox beaver hat, and wait while Gilda would replace the empty black bag with an identical full one. This scene would be repeated up and down the avenues. No one I ever knew could say whether he worked for the city, county or the mob? But it wasn't just gambling, bootlegging and prostitution that paid off. There was an inventory tax that was due the county every year. The nattily dressed assistant auditor would waddle into a clothing store, look around and give the proprietor an indication of what he expected. Then he'd return a week later, pick up a new suit, a bag of money and, oh, yes, the phony inventory sheet! The police had three levels of law, one for people of means, one for white trash and, of course, one for people of color. They found it legal to hold you in jail for three days for investigation, no charges, no phone calls. If, when they pushed you into the elevator and you fell down and got hurt, they'd keep you a couple of weeks until you healed. They did that to me when I gave the desk sergeant a lecture on democracy. But that was over a year ago and now with the Reverend in my camp, I hoped I was immune to their *special attention*. I sensed that Smithy, the juvenile detective, was nervous about really hassling me. But, he was always in there, tugging on my coat. One day, he said, baiting me, "Make it clear for me. We've all heard how fucking tough you are. But how, tell me, how are you going to whip someone like me? I'm a trained fuzz, I've been to FBI school. I'm 37 years old and I weigh 215 pounds. You're what, 17? Sure, you've got those pumped-up biceps, but what's that hung on, a 145 pound body—and that's 145 pounds if you're soaking wet!" he laughed.

"Sure, Smithy," I answered. "I'll make it clear to you. You do something that threatens my core, makes me think I need to protect myself or mine and I could find a way, maybe just mess up your hair a little." I laughed.

"Okay, then how are you going to beat my Thirty-Eight revolver?" he asked.

"Now you're making it easy; a 357 Magnum beats a Thirty-Eight every time," I answered.

"But, I'm wearing mine right over my left tit; and you, I see nothing on you?" he countered.

"Weapons are always available when the need arises. But it doesn't take anyone like me. See those two cats over at that nine-ball table? They'd be delighted to take you out. They've never even been in a rumble, but if someone gave the word, they'd see it as their calling–like a religious thing– no one could stop them, " I said.

"And you'd be minister to give them their calling?" he offered.

"No, never," I answered. "Look, I'm just philosophiz- ing here, being the Devil's advocate. I only use that force that is absolutely necessary. I'm into love. That's my calling. I don't want fear. Fear is easy to get. Any street thug or crazy cop can get you that. Those two cats over there, they love me, I speak for them, say the words they can't. I can get them this club, that library, those pool tables. Whoever supplies the most needs gets the most love. They talk about my being their leader but that's not true. I'm more their bitch, their mother. But again, I'm just philosophizing here. I have no hard feelings against you. I know you've got a wife and two kids at home. Those are good things. They come from love. I respect that. I want that someday. Meantime, it's all too busy. I've got Moon's girlfriend's Mafia father detailing his mugs to follow us every night; and I've got you sniffing around here every day. Ah, why are you worried about me, it can't be official? Answer me that, Smithy."

"I will answer you that. True, I'm not worried about you. Why would I? You're nothing but a puffed-up little pea- cock. It's your arrogance that blisters me. A whim and a wham and you're up there talking to the Mayor, even hav- ing lunch with His Honor and the Police Commissioner. Hey, I'm a Sergeant and I've never even been in he same room with of them. You're riding around in a fancy sports car and a custom Cadillac. You're taking advantage of a lot of naive, but good people. And, my *calling*, to use your word, is to catch you at it," he spit out.

"Well, when I'm guilty of some grievous offense, I hope you do catch me," I said.

"I bet you do, I just bet you do, Kid; and you can be sure I will." With that, he smiled, his big face rounding and small eyes almost closing as he did. He left.

I sat there too sick to move. I slid down in my seat. I guess my body language signaled the Reverend. He sat down opposite me. "That's a dangerous enemy you've got there, Kid."

"I know," I said, "so ignorant and so dangerous, and not just dangerous for me but for everyone." He nodded, then smiled to cheer me. "Guess he's just someone I'll have to learn to live with. Say, another dangerous man I've learned to live with–Mr. Arno, the don. What do you know about him?"

"I should hate him," he said, "but Arno is a special case. I have to say I like him a good deal. He has some wily ways. They say he can spend years, nay decades, playing mental games. And, he always wins! I just wish he was on our side, that's all."

Wondrously, the Reverend never had to be consistent. He could love someone like the don or me, though in most ways we stood for things he hated. Thanks for *deep* love and *shallow* hatred. Saintly. Still, he coveted the righteous and allowed only a few of us others in his orb.

Mary Lee was a saint of another kind. Danny Walton called her an angel with dirty feet. "She walks in the gutter with her heart in the clouds," he'd say. There was a time Moon and I couldn't get our day started without a word of counsel from her. We'd meet at the early riser coffee club at the Husk Café. We'd sit at the counter and she'd peer at us through eyes alcohol had closed only a few hours earlier, but she saw more clearly than any teatotaler. Jack Gillette, Dave Davie, Don Smith, Whitey Easting, and Frenchy Falentine were in the group. Whitey had a crush on her but he knew it couldn't come to anything. Frenchy was crazy about her and she cared deeply for him, but she had some problems that made marriage impossible, something everyone knew but Frenchy. The other people in the group were more her age but she gave her attention to Moon and me. We were her babies, she'd cradle us with her big brown eyes, while we absorbed her insights and goodness. Her touch was sensuous, every shade of beautiful. I couldn't leave for school 'til she touched me, usually on the right shoulder. That touch was telling me that I was good, too; and whatever she was saying I couldn't doubt. I'd be jealous when I saw her do the same for someone else, but then would come the pangs of guilt; I had no call, no rights. You can't lay claim to someone like that. A wino would be sitting on the curb, the residue of his recent BM plainly on his shoes. She'd give him her quarter (perhaps her last) a pat on the head, a touch on the cheek and lift him back into humanity–the gift!

Yes, *The Gift,* that's what I titled the theme paper I wrote about her. Mrs. Herring read it to the class. "Oh, eke!" one of the girls said, when Mary Lee put her hand on the drunk, but Mary Lee never had an *eke* in her. She did have a lot of pain in her, though. You could see the round, deep cigarette burns on her throat when the covering neckerchief slipped a little. The foster parent who did that to her made my father, with his alder switches, seem like Santa. She was our delicate flower, but a flower that the angry alders had cut deeply. We canonized her all the more for the scars. The foster system had left her incapable of having children, unless by way of Immaculate Conception; but Moon and I knew our mama, and we siblings had no rivalry. We each clutched one of her small breasts, content that there was enough milk for both.

Moon

Hi, it's Moon again. Now, for a quick background sketch. I was born in Tacoma General Hospital like everyone else who lived in the north end of Tacoma and wasn't Catholic. If you were Catholic you were probably hatched in St. Joseph's Hospital. My mother died giving me life. My grandmother raised me 'til she died when I was sixteen. I had never seen much of my father who was the sales manager for a large electrical firm; so there wasn't much reason to stick around home. I left when I was sixteen and went to live with the Kid in the Holly Hotel down on Eighth and Pacific. It wasn't a bad flea trap, I stayed there two years. I was okay with the streets, but I wasn't really cut out for those small hotels. Everybody's business was your own. One night Clyde, the owner, was really chewing us out for partying. He paused for a moment in his rage, when from the next room came a wild scream, then a whimper, and then, "You bit me, honey." Some of Reverend Powers' friends took me in. They were good shits. I was their little lost atheist. They had a huge house and no children, so I was no bother. There was a three-car garage with one bedroom over and one off the side. The wife had arthritis, the bad kind; so they had only one car, which they preferred to park in front to shorten her walk. They gave me the whole garage wing for a playpen – perfect. I paid them rent when I had it but they let me know it wasn't important.

Those were the three places *where* I lived–now, for *what* I lived. My given name was Raymond, Raymond Wells in full, but soon nobody ever called me either of those. My name became Moon. You see I probably invented the *Moon*. At least that's what everyone in Tacoma thinks. Myself? I certainly wouldn't swear it on a stack of sheet music. Weird, the way it happened. I was playing first saxophone in the Stadium High School Orchestra. My three heroes were Coleman Hawkins, Lester Young, and Ben Webster; but my inspiration was Corky Corcoran. He plays for Harry James, but previously he played tenor for Lincoln High. He was blown out of school for doing an unscheduled solo in a mundane spring concert. Lincoln did him a great favor; he went right from there to the James Band, where he has since been featured in all the hip progressive stuff. He was so young at the time, Harry and Betty had to adopt him so that he could tour with the band, but imagine having Betty Grable for a mamma. Corky represented for me and my group someone who had given the *finger* to authority and had won. To the school administration he was the outlaw who was going to Hell because he didn't receive that little chicken shit diploma. So when Bernie Sederic on bass, Bobbie Woodhouse on piano, and me on the sax were working up a little riff, minutes before our spring concert was to begin, I was unashamedly acting up. I'd swing the sax above my right shoulder, then drop it down to my left knee, when all of a sudden the acid tongued music director popped through the wings, mike in hand. "Hey, Raymond, who do you think you are, Corky Corcoran?" Well, there were already a lot of people there, maybe two hundred, mostly cats–friends. There was a hush to see what I'd do. I was wearing dark blue gabardines and no shorts. (No shorts was a popular fad, we'd have quick draw contests in the locker room to see who could be ready for the chicks the quickest.) Anyway, what got into me, I don't know? I whipped off my saxophone, spun–then like the quickest gun in the west, I dropped my slacks, put both palms on the floor, and turned two beautiful cheeks to the music director. The cheers, the applause and the laughter were spiritual! I was an instant hero, and famous beyond imagining. I was also kicked out of school. Too bad too, it was my junior year and Stadium still had some things I wanted. We all scoffed at the music department because it seemed a step back from the experience we had had with Delwin Jones at Mason Junior High, but it was helpful nonetheless. And, a sculpture I had done for Mrs. Benson's art class had made the cut and would have been up for honors at the state art festival. And fuck, I'd had the third fastest time in cross-country–as a senior it would have been all mine!

Once out of school, my music didn't stick. I don't know. I tried out for a couple of bands; I'd hit some good shit. I knew how to avoid melodies using unusual cord harmonies. I had speed and power. They liked me, they encouraged me, but it didn't come together. Perhaps I wanted too much, I'd just turned seventeen. Anyway from then on it was just Moon, Mooner, Moonbeam–my first last and middle name. Ah, I could sit in on some jams, briefly. Dick Morehead would say, "Come on up here, Moon! Pick up that sax, Cat." But I knew he just wanted to have a little fun with me, not exactly at my expense because they did like to see, and have their audience see me frolic with the horn–do one or two of my pat routines and then fake a Moon. I'd just flip my suit coat up in the back, put both hands on the floor, and they'd

cheer. Christ, how they'd cheer. Actually I never had to do
another true Moon. Get it right once. Quit. After the cheers,
I'd bow out. Of course it would allow me to pick the sweetest little chick on the dance floor. Good time Moon–he plays,
he dances, and he shows his sweet cheeks. Sure, I wasn't
going anywhere, but I was having a great time bopping in
place.

Bop was our music. Be-bop was the altar on which
we lit our candles. We laughed at Louis Armstrong. Dizzy
Gillespie and Charlie Parker were gods. Glen Miller had been
dead for over five years. The Dorsey Brothers were looking
for caskets. For us, "big band" meant Kenton, Ellington, and
Basie. Oh yeah, we'd dig Woodie Herman as one of his Herds
stampeded across the stage. But, Kenton was our clear favorite. He had audacity; he stripped vibrato from his vocals,
brought in elements of classical music and just generally
pounded us senseless with his all powering sound. He kept
spinning off new stars like Rugulo, Getz, Mann, and
Ferguson. And, they all came through the Puget Sound. You
could catch them at the Trianon in Seattle, the Century in
Tacoma, or the Evergreen in Olympia. Sometimes for a
Kenton, a Hampton, or a Krupa we'd get a group together
and make all three. About half the night would be devoted
to dancing, the remaining part we'd just stand around listening, concert style, but we'd participate too with shouts
like *Go Man, go!* and *Work, work, work it Daddy!* There
would be Stan Kenton at the piano; he'd cut to Shelly Mann
on the drums. Shelly would rate a five minute solo, then he'd
hand it to Maynard Ferguson on the trumpet, and Fergie's
horn would retract your eardrums as his trumpet hit the high-
est note your flappers had ever heard. Then June Christy,

the Queen of Cool, would come on so soft you'd again have to retune your ear. After a couple of ballads, she'd blow you away with "How High the Moon"! She'd lift you so high with love for her, love for Kenton, and love for jazz. There were no fights when Kenton came to the Century Ballroom, zero—two thousand cats, 1000 white, 700 boot, 300 Mex and no fights—a miracle! I guess they had other nourishment that night. Why such nourishment came from Kenton and Christy, I could never say. Neither always hit every note right on as a Basie or an Ella might have, and neither looked the part—not polished and slick like so many musicians. Kenton was tall, really tall; you could more imagine him with a basketball than a piano. And Christy, she looked shy, like the sweet virgin just about to say "yes," but stepping back just in time so she always remained pure. Kid said their flaws gave us a peek at their souls—let us love them more. I don't know, but I too, adored them.

It wasn't all music however; we could get up a softball game on any weekend with good weather. In the summer we could take a couple of cars and go on a week's cruise and crash every church picnic, or those for the Sons of Ireland, Sons of Montana—you name it! Tacoma is surrounded by lakes (Hi-dive at Surprise Lake was the greatest), and when we got tired of fresh water, we could take a dip in salt water at Point Defiance Beach or cross the Sound to Burton on Vashon Island. But Point Defiance always had the Sons of Norway picnic—that was our summer ritual. The Norwegians were naive and generous—wonderful, and we'd acquired a taste for those sweet blondes. Jefferson, this boot cat that hung with us, said to me, "Moon, what part of Norway am I suppose to be from?" rubbing his kinky hair.

"I don't know," I said, "ask the Kid, he's a square head."

"Bergen, tell them you're from Bergen," Kid answered. "And, say that your second cousin, once-removed, still writes to you. That will keep them from asking any more questions." It worked too. Jeffers would say the words and they'd fix him another helping of grilled salmon and pour him another glass of Heidelberg.

Moon

They called us cats–the cat gang. That was okay, we called ourselves cats. I think the image was of a clean, well dressed predator, who calmly waits, never getting up a sweat, and nails every sweet thing that comes along–well, something like that. Of course he digs music and wears outrageously cool threads. Our gang was kind of a loose thing. We could call five to six hundred together at our prime. We had 273 members in the Ultra Club. (Ultra meant ultra hip.) That was the club the Kid set up to run the youth center. One day out of the blue, Kid goes to the City Council and gives a speech on Tacoma's need for a youth center. The Reverend Powers, who ran the influential Council of Churches, got behind him as did the mayor who had a choice piece of property for rent. The next thing anyone knew they set aside the room overlooking Pacific Avenue in the mayor's own bowling complex, free of charge. (Of course the city had to pick up the expenses.) The only stipulation to us was that it had to be run as a formal club–officers, accounts, Robert's rule, etc. And *voila'*, the Ultra Club was born, and the youth center was its charge.

We were at once respectable. City, county, and state agencies would come by; Kid would get a group of us to pose with them, and the next day our picture would be in the *News Tribune*. Social workers would come by and they sent a grad student from as far away as the University of

Washington. We kept booze and drugs out so there were never any hassles, and truly that was what all the cats wanted, a clean place uncontaminated by booze and drugs where you could lay back, put your suedes on some comfortable furniture, and not be troubled by uptight adults. But the Kid never stopped. His testes are about the size of Mount Rainier. One day he says, "I think I'll go to City Hall and pick up some money for a library." A week later, count 'em, seven days, and I'm carrying a set of *Encyclopedia Britannica* up the long staircase, plus a set of *World Classics*, fifty distinguished novels, and an eight-inch thick dictionary. I was dubbed the "librarian." Cats donated books by the dozen. I kept everything that didn't look stolen. I even found a copy of the *Bawdy Dictionary for 1960*. Never mind that 1960 hadn't arrived yet, it was so off the wall. You could lookup "slut," and it would give you the definition you'd expect, but then when it used it in a sentence it would throw in a little humor. It said, "A slut is the kind of girl you want to take home to mother, that is if your mom is a hooker." The books were instantly put to use. I even saw the Reverend using the reference books. But we had heated discussions, and that's where they were really employed.

Next, the Kid wangled us a huge jukebox, a great red, white, and blue monster that contained 350 selections and had wonderful speakers, six of them. He said he bought it for almost nothing from that old WWII USO up on Fawcett Avenue. As president he appointed himself Music Director; so, of course, it was loaded with Webster, Hampton, Kenton, Christy, and Eckstine. That's where his nickels went, but as librarian, I had the keys; so I could change the records and lift the coins when the need arose – mostly for parties. It was our slush fund, no accounting in the club books.

Moon

As I said, we had some rousing discussions. "Wrangling," the Reverend used to call it. I'd call the Kid a musical moron and he'd call me an esoteric twerp. Truly, Kid wasn't educated in music; he wouldn't know a sharp from a flat. But he knew what he liked, and what he liked was great music–I guess that's what you call taste. I mean he introduced me to Sonny Stitt, Dexter Gordon, and Ben Webster when he was barely fifteen. Where or how he picked up on shit like that in raggedy-ass'd little Tacoma, I'll never understand. I do think once he heard something even once, he held it. It was his.

Many of our discussions were about religion. The Council of Churches had quarters in our building, and they had this cutesy little chapel set right between the lunch counter and the youth center hall. It was there for atmosphere and of course their weekly meetings, which were all of one hour a week. The remaining time we used it for a quiet study, a place for private talks, or just to have fun with little Susie. No, we didn't have any real sex there, that was out of bounds just like booze and drugs.

It stimulated some pretty outrageous theological discussions, too. Kid and I were both atheists as you might have gathered. Oh, we had differences; he called himself an Emerging Evolutionist. He explained it something like this: Since the whole is greater than the sum of its parts, the soul could exist outside the whole in the *greater,* or some such place. Looking at it another way: if a billion people could imagine it, it existed if in no other place than in their imagining, because imaginings are real, too. You can't say a person didn't imagine what he had just imagined! It all sounded like a big stretch to me but still fun to kick around. Had he believed that the soul was just the deep recesses of the mind, that would have been acceptable, but that was not what he envisioned. My philosophy rides on the sharp edge of Ockham's Razor: Cut out anything that isn't necessary. And a soul wasn't necessary to explain anything I'd seen in this world. I explained myself as a raw atheist. I had no mind to sugarcoat anything. A few others in the group felt like we did, but most had no opinions–the rest were theists. Buz Weatley, my clarinetist buddy, was a true Catholic and he'd come at me in so many proselytizing ways. He finally exasperated me; so one day I said, "Buz, you're talking to me again about God. And, you know my opinions on the subject; so you must want the core of my thinking. Is that right?"

"Please," he said in his sweet, disarming way. I had the *Bawdy Dictionary* on my knee. It's a sizable book with a fake leather cover. It could almost be mistaken for a Bible from a distance. I knew Buz would respect its appearance. I began to bandy it about.

"Words have meaning, even nasty words, wouldn't you agree, Buz?" He nodded. "And the meanings are right here in this dictionary, right in this." I opened it to the last page, "Right in these 1226 pages. Any off-colored word you can think of is perfectly explained in this considerable work." He began to scrutinize the dictionary, but I pulled it back. "And sometimes, naughty or not, the off color word is just right. Wouldn't you agree, Buz?" He nodded again. "Now Buz, you know that old, ugly refugee joke?" He shook his head, *no*. I begin in my stupid accent, having fun with it.

"I'm a cut a hair by the dozens, and no a body calls-za me a *barbeer.* I'm a paint-ta pictures by da grossa, and no a body calls me an a *arteest.*" Buz starts to laugh a little. I jump up and pantomime the playing of a violin. "I'm a play a my a fiddle at all a dances, and no a body calls a me a *musician.*" Now Buz is really laughing. I pause, grabbing his leg to get his full attention. "An a now a I'm a suck a one cock and the whole world a calls me a *cocksuckieer!*" I open the dictionary and mock read, "'The oral copulation of the male sex organ, but in bawdy language, one who commits an unimaginable offense against one of his fellows. Be aware that *once a cocksucker always a cocksucker;* he can't change, because, as we all know, *lost innocence can never be retrieved!*' It says so right here." I point to the page.

"Now," I pause, 'Imagine, Buz, if you will? There's this cool cat; he's the greatest in the entire universe. He's a combination of Bird, Diz, Getz, and Kenton. And now, this great cat creates in his own image, of course, this wimpish little square-john; and this *omniscient* cat says to him, "I created you and that's a great honor for a pusillanimous piece of dreck like you. So, to be worthy you've got to love me. No. More! You've got to worship me, but that's just the beginning; here's a book full of commandments. I demand that you do these things, if you don't I'll cast you down to Hell. There you'll experience all manner of torture, fire, and brimstone. This brimstone, a gross sulfur smell, will permeate the chaos and stifle your every move. But, be assured, if you worship me to my satisfaction I'll lift you to Heaven, my house. Still, be aware, if you don't behave I'll still send you to Hell, which will hurt doubly because you'll have known my lofty company."

"Now, that's some heavenly cat! Would you and that fine horn of yours jam with a cat like that? Naw, you'd give him the finger and call him, a what? A tyrant? A villain? A despot? No, those erudite, but puny words won't do. (Buz shakes his head in agreement.) We'll have to go to the *Bawdy Dictionary* for the right word." I quickly open the book, desperately thumbing the pages for the exact word. "Here's one, *prick*. I again pretend to read, "'One who commits an unimaginable offense against his fellows.' Hey, that's familiar. But wait, it says here a prick may do a dastardly deed today, but tomorrow he may soften and change. Oh, goodness, *prick* simply won't do because he can change. Let's go back to *cocksucker*." Again I wildly search. Ah, ah, it does have the same meaning. Except, as you'll remember, he can't change because once a cocksucker, always a cocksucker! His innocence is irretrievable! You see, don't you, Buz? God *is* a cocksucker!!"

"Buz, Buz, come back. You've forgotten your clarinet!"

Kid

I did some thinking about Smithy. The best I could come up with was "Out of sight, out of mind;" so I simply called the station, found the times of his shifts, and made certain I wasn't at the Center during those periods. He slipped to a back pocket on the old one-ball table. That actually helped give more time for Abby, my first full involvement with a girl. I needed a little air because I was still working my shine parlor, and I was consumed with reading. Mrs. Herring, my Lit teacher, had given me Socrates, Cervantes, and Whitman. It was like Moon and me passing on jazz records, "Here listen to these and you'll be cool."

Mrs. Herring would say, "Here read this and you'll be hip." She knew a lot of jazz talk. Her son, Billy Herring, was a drummer friend of mine, three years my senior, who was lost to horse, that's what we called heroin. Billy and I had met at the pool hall and had many laughs picking on one another. I told him he was just a country bumpkin with two stupid matching sticks who loved to hang around jazz musicians.

He countered with "And this from a pug who has had more canvas on his back than Tacoma Tent and Awning!" Of course, meaning I'd been knocked down so often in the ring. I knew Mrs. Herring grieved for Billy and I was some kind of a link, a role I was privileged to play. When she gave me Hemingway's *A Farewell to Arms,* I read it in one sitting.

Hemingway spoke to me like no one else: the good die young, the big words that moved people to self-destruction; show me someone who repeatedly uses the word *integrity* and I'll show you someone who hasn't any. I must admit I like concepts like loyalty to friends (not Country) but don't talk about it, just do it quietly. At the same time, screw all the flags that all the Betsy Rosses in all the world can sew! Anyway when I was not in a book, Moon's chick, Babs was pulling me to an art museum. I fell in love with the Impressionists and Post-Impressionists. I thought the Giverny district in France was the coolest place on Earth. I selected a print called *The Idlers* and hung it on my wall in the Holly Hotel. Clyde, the owner, said, "This place has no pretense for culture."

So I'd just say, "She sure has nice tits!"

I got rid of the shine parlor. Not that I didn't want the money, but there was simply no time. I had done well with the little enterprise. Shoeshines were bringing only a quarter, but the State liquor stores were closed at ten p.m.; so any time after that you could get six dollars for a $2.58 pint of Old Rocking Chair. That doubled my income on the weekends. All right, I felt guilty about it, but I rationalized that I was helping out, after all, the State wasn't taking care of business. Oh, yeah, I'd slip Tiny, the beat cop, a pint when he got his free shine. So with the $400 received from the shine stand and the $1260 I had in my cedar cigar box, I knew I wasn't going to be left out in the cold. My room was only twelve dollars a week. I didn't need wheels; my chick had a Morgan 4+4, meaning it had four wheels (earlier ones had only three) and that it could seat four, which was cool for such a small car. It was British racing green with black leather belts over the hood. We exercised it regularly. Her dad, a sports car buff, sported a silver Aston Martin, a black Cadillac Allard, and a blue Cadillac four door. The Allard was the wickedest thing in town–a full race, two-seater with cycle fenders. It weighed about 2500 pounds and had a 300-hp Cadillac engine. If you really stood on it and weren't ready it could be like a bicycle on ice. Abby and I used to crank it on Fog Alley. That was everyone's favorite drag strip near the abandoned Navy warehouses in Lakewood. Moon had his old pot that we used to drive sometimes, but mostly it was so ugly he kept it hidden. He did drive it to work at Tacoma Screw Products. (Moon loved that name.) In the evening you'd see him in Bab's white Cadillac phaeton which she had inherited from her mom. It was a rare four-door convertible with custom everything–chrome spoked wheels, white rolled and pleated leather interior with an ebony and gold dashboard. Its chassis was only six inches longer than normal, but somehow they found room for a hi-fi, a bar, and picnic tables. You'd push a button, pull a lever and they'd pop right out. Equally impressive was the solid gold plaque on the dash, "Built exclusively for Barbara Arno."

Moon

There were two factions in the club; first the music people who loved to sing, dance, and listen to tunes; second, the street fighter people who were necessary as they provided safe passage. There were, of course, wannabes to both groups. They were also useful, like when three cats were beaten on McKinley Hill. The Kid took 515 guys up there, maybe 200 of them wannabes. I think everyone went except me. They lined both sides of the street and the tops of all the buildings. When it came to a head to head meeting, it turned out to be the Kid meeting two old boxing buddies, Dave Rooney and Eddie Marsh–good guys. There was no fight and we never had to show force like that again.

There were lots of crossovers; of course the Kid was a prime example. When he had a good partner and was really feeling the tunes, we'd all step aside and watch him dance. Man, he was light on his feet; people said it was from boxing, but I knew it was just him. He had had great promise as a welterweight, but then one day he just walked away. Even I never knew why. Everyone was disappointed, "But it's his life," they'd say.

The truth is that if he never had another fight he'd be happy. He told me one night that fighting was what kids do; "They call me Kid so I go on swinging." I'm certain he's outgrown it, but we won't let him quit. Kid once said that I could be a fighter. I was intrigued. Anyone who can dance, can fight, can make love. They all require the same skills–rhythm, coordination, courage, and to be great, a dash of madness. (I'd have said: can dance, can fight, can fuck.) But, as it stands, I'm no fighter; so when some bad cat wants to punch me out I say "I'm a lover not a fighter," and if that doesn't work, I say "the Kid handles all my light work." Then the Kid pumps that right of his a time or two and I'm out of there, homefree– no bumps, no bruises.

The bad dudes say, "Kid is short but he carries a mean load with him. Moon is tall but he carries a mean Kid with him." Okay, I know it's not fair, but he's there for fuck's sake and I can't help using him, too. He is our seminal cat–our seed that creates new ideas, new strength, new freedom. We stand behind his shield. He lacks the fear that so often paralyzes the rest of us, especially me. I'd see him getting into it with some animal. I'd say, "Hey, Bra that cat's big, bad and ugly, and he has two friends if he's not enough. How you going to handle that much meat?"

He put his hand on my shoulder and forced eye contact (something I always found difficult) and said, "Sure I could walk away, but then I'd be giving up some of my street. I'd be giving up some of my freedom. I've done that a time or two and I didn't like it. Now, as to 'managing that big animal' I never know. There are no guaranties. But, I've the confidence I'll find a way. I'm no fool, I know someday I'll lose, but not tonight. I've won, what would you say forty-four maybe forty-five times in a row? Now, wouldn't it be weak to think it wouldn't happen the forty-sixth time? And, if I ever think it won't happen for me this time, will I ever be able to believe it will happen for me again?"

It did happen for him that night. I was holding Kid's

sports coat. The animal lunged at him; Kid sidestepped, caught the cat's index finger with his left, fully extending it. The big guy froze in mid-step. Kid's right hand took the finger as a waiter would a corkscrew and twisted until the cat's jaw was grinding on the sidewalk, his leg high in the air in a hopeless attempt at counterbalance. As his two friends slowly, but malevolently advanced, Kid's eyes focused on the finger. All eyes followed his. Then with a flourish, he popped it! That held them. I saw one guy swallow his Adam's apple. Next he took the quivering guy's ring finger in that same right hand; he motioned for them to leave. They were understandingly accommodating. After, we drove the big fellow up the hill to Pierce County Hospital. He rode quietly.

"Shit!" I said, when the cat got out, "You're that dammed idiot from La Mancha, a fucking knight errant swinging those mitts of yours at useless windmills!"

"No, " he laughed, "I'm that dammed Dapple, his knaves ass, giving sweet idiots like you a fun ride." It was maddening to argue with the Kid, as soon as you were certain you had won some points, he'd hit you with a reversal. I mean, I'd just read Cervantes. I knew Quixote's horse was Rosinante; but, fuck, who keeps track of his servant's donkey? He, also, hit me on the arm and it hurt for a week.

Moon

The Kid talks about the "Song of the Street." He never fully articulated it but I'm certain I know what he means. He'd say you could sense the tune developing, but you could never predict how it would play out. Me? I'd watch the streets throw up a group of characters like notes on sheet music with its flats and sharps, its majors and minors; then float a rhythm through it with its confounding patterns of emphasis and duration. Last, it would be hammered by a riff that says, "I'll kill you if you don't watch out." The riff would be repeated 'til you ignored it; and then it would have you.

Picture the Palmer brothers setting out from some hovel in the Salishan housing project, beer in hand, looking for some heads to crack, overconfident in their ability–not hearing the riff. Now, comes three of the Sixth Army's elite who had helped take Hill Four during last week's bivouac. They, too, are ignoring the riff. They are headed for the 1306 Cabaret, where the largest of them had met a foxy lady named Mary Lee. All she had done was allow him to buy her a whisky sour, but he had taken it as a promise of something more. Then comes Clyde the cop, who's also a professional wrestler–two hundred and fifty-five pounds of muscle and meanness, backed up by pair of handcuffs, an oversized Billy club, and a 38 caliber revolver. Nasty as he is, he still has protective feelings for Mary Lee. Then there's Frenchy Falentine, the former middleweight contender. He throws fist so fast they call him "The Blur." He thinks he's going to marry Mary Lee.

Watch, now come the Palmer brothers through the cut glass door of the 1306. They holler something fresh at Mary Lee. Frenchy flexes, but remains on his stool. It's 8:33 and Mary Lee is just finishing her third whiskey sour, it's sustaining her, but just barely. The soldiers enter and the big one shouts, "Set up one more whiskeeey for Mary Leee from Tennesseee!" Now, Mary Lee is a caregiver, she gives to the weak and the helpless, and right now Frenchy on her right is trying to see how he can get through another night without his beloved. The silver plate the Navy had installed in his head is throbbing, his thick neck is bulging under his knit tie, his face is crimson; and Mary Lee is consoling him, her right hand innocently resting on his thigh. The soldier throws a ten on the counter; the bartender sweeps it, as he gives Mary Lee her fresh drink. She tips the drink to the soldier, thanking him for helping her sustain. The soldier, now having bought her two drinks is feeling proprietary rights. He looks down seeing her hand on Frenchy. Blind rage lifts his hands towards her small neck, but Frenchy is called to do what he is trained for as his left hook breaks the big soldier's nose; then the right meets the jaw and the soldier is cold on the floor. His two buddies attempt a rescue. One is driven to the floor, but the second breaks a beer pitcher over Frenchy's skull. Clyde, the cop, is at the door now. Frenchy is on one knee, then Mary Lee with full heart leaps to his assistance, but he hurls her aside, crushes the last soldier, and now losing all humanity, kicks the first Palmer brother, then falls on the other with murderous lefts and rights. That's when Clyde's big, black club from high above, pushed by a 58 inch chest and an 18 inch bicep finds the skull separating it from the silver plate the Navy surgeons had so cleverly installed. World War II had finally ended for Frenchy, but it was still blazing for Mary Lee as she prostrates herself over the fallen Frenchy.

"Don't touch him!" she screams, as Clyde attempts to take his pulse.

She removes his tie placing her face on his neck. Her undulating body gives Frenchy's corpse the act so long denied. Her orgasm was long and horrifying for the spellbound spectators. When at last she slips off, her blank eyes meet the bartender's.

"Don't touch him," she says. Then to the bouncer at door, "Don't touch him!" Then to the Salvation Army conductor on the corner of Thirteenth, "Don't touch him!" Then to Long John Silver at the corner of Eleventh she whispers, "Don't touch him."

. . . .

The kid, Whitey, me, and about 200 others gathered at the Tacoma Athletic Club for the wake. His Honor the mayor, Big John Anderson, and Don Arno sat together for once, propriety having lost all significance. I could never imagine Whitey crying, but there he was. There was so much loss, and so much love present. I've been to wakes where there was much gaiety. "Celebrating the life," they'd say; but I never saw the faintest smile at this one! Danny Walton, sports editor of the *News Tribune*, gave the eulogy. I picked up a copy:

"We are here to commemorate the lives of two beloved people, Frenchy Falentine and Mary Lee Travis–both champions, but not the ones you'll find in reference books. One was the greatest fighter I've known, with a soul to match–the other, the sweetest spirit life has given. The ravages of a molested childhood deprived her of the ability to be the woman Frenchy craved. For every measure of pain that had been inflicted on her, she reversed and returned it in love–in love and caring. She fed the poor and coddled the weary. She could not help but love Frenchy. His pain, that had won him the Navy Cross, was present every waking moment in his handsome but tortured face. God will pardon his combat exuberance that saved his buddies lives. God will pardon his use of a lethal fist in defense of his love. God will pardon her alcoholic escape. God will pardon her unlawful exit. But, we will never pardon this God that allowed this to happen."

Fuck...

Moon

The Kid and I were the only ones with true monikers; I guess that's the right word, nickname doesn't seem quite right. Sure, there was Little Bill and Fat Frank, but these nicknames were tied to their given names, and you didn't often use them in their presence. Ours were all there was, our real names forgotten, we couldn't escape them! I'd walk into a club with a small group playing, even if they were old guys, and they'd strike up "Moon over Miami." I'd have to go on stage and do my schtick. Sometimes I hated it, but I never refused. I'm positive that's how the Kid handled it, too. Perhaps that is part of our bond.

For a good while, we had another bond. I fell hard for Babs–this cute little artsy Italian chick, and Kid liked her more than we cared to admit. Fortunately, she had this girlfriend, Abby. They were both short, stacked, and outrageous. "A" and "B", Abby and Babby we called them. Babs had short, jet black hair–Sicilian. Abby had long, golden blond hair–Nordic. For nine months, the length of a pregnancy, we lived in a hippodrome, round and around the chariots flew– never stopping, hardly slowing for changes in direction. And we all seemed to be pulling in different ways; who ever wanted it most, won. And everything we did was a winner; there were no bad times. Babs created these gorgeous dolls. Otherwise her taste in art was eclectic. In the morning, she might drag us to a flower show, that evening she just happened to have four tickets to an opera in Seattle. And skiing, she was the great snowball. Little, but super coordinated, she loved to bully us on the slopes. Neither Kid nor I had ever taken time to learn how to ski; they weren't teaching that on the streets. She'd teach us a bit, but mostly make fun of us; we liked it that way. Abby's folks were into the country club scene. They had that quiet, old Tacoma money that surrounded American Lake with mansions, some the size of City Hall. Abby loved to drag us through them, at the same time showing off her radically dressed friends to the Harris tweed set. They were cautiously amused. Abby's uncle called out, "Where were you fellows during the 'Cat Riots' last year?"

The Kid, breaking into his shadow boxing routine, called out, "Ducking lefts and rights!" That was good for the laugh of the evening.

The Kid always wanted to get us on the water, rain or shine. On a lark he had learned to sail in the Junior Program which gave him long term access to a fleet of beater Lake Washington flatties; and we'd spend hours sailing them. Babs, like on the ski slope, would get to laughing and try to crash them. Had I not grabbed the tiller a time or two, I swear someone would have died. After, Babs would take us by her dad's sailboat, moored at the yacht club. Just looking at it set off some dreams; I guess we just enjoyed rubbing up against it because the skipper offered to take us out any time we wanted, but we never went. Kid did once on his own, though.

When I picked the outing it was always music oriented; my monomania, I guess. The musician's picnic at Lake Wilderness was my finest coup–two days of chaos with two thousand musicians and music freaks from the greater Seattle-Tacoma area. You'd expect to see performers like Chuck Streach, Dick Morehead, Neil Friel, Bill Ramsey, Buzzy Bridgeford, Traff Hubert, Jimmy Gilles, Snuffy Smith, Freddie Greenwell, maybe Don Lanphere would be over from Wenatchee, and even a light like Corky Corcoran would probably be on leave for the summer mayhem. They had a big band stand where a new group would set up every hour or so. The big band era where 2500 bands were on tour was over, but there didn't seem to be any shortage in our area. They also had a dance pavilion where small groups would jam. Freddie, Traff, and Gilles from the Pirates' Cove would set up shop there. The brewers and the unions co-sponsored the event; so you could sample iced tubs of Heidelberg, Rainier, and Olympia, plus tables overflowing with hors d'oeuvres. Any cat who had any pretense of being hip had to be there. When it came to dancing they loved the four of us. We'd get wild, wild as you could and still not be in jail. We had worked up a routine for a foursome at the youth center, and we laid it on them. Babs and Abby had training in both ballet and gymnastics and could do some tricky shit, while Kid and I added some off the wall moves. For our finale, Babs and I did a deep dip; Abby hit her splits right on with her head on her knee and her hair sweeping the floor, and Kid did his Statue of Liberty with the heavy foot on my shoulder and the light one on Abby's head. We killed them!

After, we crowded into Abby's little Morgan just as the King County Sheriff arrived. The top was down and the wind buffeted our faces, Babs fell asleep on my shoulder. It was heaven just lending her my shoulder; I felt I gave her so little while she just gave and gave. She knew intuitively what I felt, wanted, needed. She spent at least an hour every after-

noon working with her dolls. It was like music practice had
been for me. Just watching her was special for me, and she
made me know I belonged there. I was certain of our relationship; it would be forever–no doubts there. What would
get me down was how was I going to support her? She had
so much. She drove around in a goddamn Cadillac phaeton
for pity's sake; so I could get down. She'd walk by, seemingly paying no attention to this moody lump, and when I
least expected it, she'd reach back, run her index finger over
my lips, swing behind me, roughly bite my ear; and then
without pausing she'd be right back painting her dolls, leaving me content to know I was the luckiest cat in the universe.

"There's the Buick," Abby said looking in the rear
view mirror.

"Yes, yes," the Kid said turning his head, "it's reas-
suring they'd find us way out here in the sticks!"

We were always followed, or as the Kid said, "escorted" by a '49 Buick four door. Babs' father, it was common knowledge, was don to the local Mafia. He could control everything else, but he couldn't control Babs, no one
could. Controlling Babs was the last thing I wanted to do, I
just wanted to keep up with her excitement. I was so intoxi-
cated with her. Her drinking did scare me, though. She'd
say some strange things under the influence, so I'd steer her
away from booze as best I could. My big trick was to drink
her drink when she wasn't looking. If she caught me I'd laugh
and say "My sauce, your loss." Trouble was I'd get drunk,
but it was still okay; she'd dutifully stay sober to take care of
me. But she'd always have the last word because later when
this sloppy drunk was trying to get her into bed she'd cheer-

fully say, "You booze, you lose," laugh and then push me away.

The other thing that scared me was the '49 Buick. Kid would say, "Look at it as back-up; they are there to protect his daughter not to hurt us. They could have taken us out long ago." Still, I was the one sitting next to his daughter. What if I fell out of favor? Mr. Arno seemed a quiet, cultured man, but there had to be some cunning for him to get where he was. He liked the Kid, that was obvious. Perhaps we were the lesser of certain evils. His wife had died five years earlier, and Babs was all he had left. He doted on her, and she played him; at least she thought she did. She made herself indispensable by being hostess at his many dinner parties. She carried it off with all the poise of a forty-year woman. I went to three, no four, and had a ball–anyone could be there: a prosecuting attorney, a bishop, a union leader, a fight promoter, hell I even saw the governor there! They occupied the entire first floor of the Bay Towers; that tall apartment building above Stadium High overlooking the Sound. There was a restaurant-sized kitchen, complete with a chef, a pastry cook, and two servers. Babs floated over them like a butterfly, always getting exactly what she wanted. After one party in honor of Babs' aunt–her substitute mama and her chaperone, we all piled into gray Cad sedans and were hustled off to the New Yorker. Mr. Arno's soldiers muscled in and set up a long, long table in front of the band. An antique, *horned* Victrola was placed on the piano and began piping out Caruso's "Come back to Sorrento." Babs explained that it had been her mom's favorite song. My friend, the great Bill Ramsey, was there leaning on his saxophone with an amused look on his face, letting me know he had seen it all before.

The New Yorker as usual, had been enjoying a packed house, but most anxious patrons soon found convenient exits. Presently Mr. Arno squelched the Victrola, asking Bill to play "Route 66" for Auntie's 66th birthday. Babs pushed me out on the dance floor with the aunt. It was an honor. She is perhaps the kindest and most gentle person I've ever met. And, she's a great little hoofer. We did a couple flashy turns and a dip at which the family wildly applauded. It was bitchin'. Babs and her father joined us for the next number, which was of course, "Come back to Sorrento" now wonderfully jazzed up by Ramsey and company. After, the don dropped some money in the Victrola horn. It was soon overflowing as the band continued to play Sorrento all night long, they knew where the magic came from. It was all magic to me.

It was all magic to the Kid, too. We'd talked about it just once; we didn't want to spook it. But we had to wonder, "Why us?" Here we were a few months ago, victims of the street, now we were its heroes. And, in particular, why me? No one had been as low as me. Kid had his shine parlor. I had nothing, but I couldn't always sponge off him. For awhile I was lucky to get one meal out of three. Then Whitey Easting, the great pool hustler, took me under his wing. I became his shill. Whitey had a big wad of tens he'd show off. He'd pretend to be a drunken sailor, we'd be playing nine ball, and I'd be beating his pants off. Anyone could see I was no great player, and they'd all be watching Whitey throw those tens at me. "I'm in," they'd say. Next thing there would be two or three new players and I'd tip-toe out. When it was over Whitey's wad would be a lot thicker. It was fun, but it was embarrassing at the same time. Then I found a job at Tacoma Screw Products and shortly after met Babs. Next, I picked up on my new pad and was atop Mount Rainier looking down on the plebes. Unlike me, the Kid never looked back, but for me the question kept coming, "Why me?" I knew it was nothing I'd earned.

Kid said you always could expect more than you deserved; if we got what we deserved we'd all get the shit kicked out of us. That, of course, couldn't work because the earth would be inundated with shit, the human race being what it is. Even this fucked-up world couldn't survive that. Well, that isn't exactly what he said, but that's what he meant. I had the idea that people had to earn respect. "No," he said, "you grant everyone respect without waiting to see if they earn it. That's the key to a quality life. If everyone is a suspect until he proves his innocence, what a tortuous world it would be. If they prove false there's plenty of time to cut them loose."

Moon

Late that winter, by coincidence, we all had birthdays a couple of weeks apart. It was their senior year, and they would all be eighteen. I was the old guy, I would be nineteen, and my birthday was last. Our idea, I think it was Abby that actually came up with it, was that the birthday person was to treat–was to be the giver.

The Kid was first; he took us to a Billy Eckstine concert. Billy started to sing, "Everything I Have Is Yours." He is a handsome son of a bitch; and about the time he hit "yours," his arms were stretched side to side; he lifted his shoulders slightly; and the women came out of their seats, down the isles, screaming. But, Billy, without missing a count said, "Steady, girls!" That was the coolest move I had ever seen. They were back in their seats and the concert continued. After, Kid took us to dinner at the China Pheasant, a roadhouse where Wardell Grey was holding court. We were told Eckstine might put in an appearance, but only a couple of his sidemen showed. After dessert, Kid presented us with stylized ceramics of our respective cars. They were dazzling, even my old pot.

Abby's treat was to take us to Longacres Night at the country club. It was billed as "Gambling for Charity." She gave us an envelope containing $69–her big joke. The place was decorated like the back room of the Turf Smoke Shop with a big, lighted board that could pace the horses just as they had done in the actual race. The event of the evening was going to be a re-run of an obscure *Longacres' Mile*. It was comical; most of the older people were certain they could remember the actual winner, but no two seemed to remember the same horse. Abby's dad remembered; so Abby, Babs, and Kid all followed him. I didn't believe him; still I knew there would be someone who knew. There was. I saw Whitey there all dressed in a black tux, running a black jack table. He swore me to secrecy, then whispered, "Pure Velvet." When the lights went out on the big board, it was Velvet by a nose; I seemed to be the only winner and I had $249 in my pocket. For the rest of the evening Abby's folks hosted a square dinner in one of the side rooms. We were joined by about twenty of Abby and Babs' friends from Aquinas High. Albert Rhubarb and his Merry Men filled the bandstand. They also filled our ears with their insipid sound. Even so, we found much to enjoy, especially me with my $249 bucks.

Babs decided for her treat, she'd give us a party at her place. She hired Buz's quartet–clarinet, piano, drums and bass. Buz encouraged me to bring my sax. The three of us, Abby, Kid, and me were seated at their huge walnut dining table, when Mr. Arno walked Babs in with a flourish as though he were presenting the bride. I trembled. Do I deserve this? I couldn't talk. I reached for my tenor and found my speech in its wondrous voice. I was on my knees playing first, "I Love You for Sentimental Reasons," not for its music, but for its fine message. I finished with our theme, "Once." "Once and Only Once the one and only comes along. Once you took my hand and ..." Ah, the lyrics. Buz took the second chorus while we kissed. No one had to tell me this was that "Once." Babs brought out three sets of dolls, all in perfect likeness of the four of us. When you removed their costumes, you found them completely detailed underneath. She must have worked every night on them. We were all teary eyed for the beauty and love she had put into them. I wondered if they were the image of the soul the Kid speaks of? If I were a theist, I'd say God got it right just this once. The dinner looked wonderful; I can't say I tasted much; I was in a dream. Her aunt, the wonderful chaperone that no one ever saw, appeared at one o'clock. Abby and Babs jumped up, hugged and kissed her, and then she disappeared again. When we left at two-thirty, Babs was quietly crying, but I was used to that when she was feeling fulfilled.

When I got to my pad, I had a driving passion to go back; but I knew it wouldn't be cool. I fought it. I wasn't sleepy; so I sat sipping some of Papa Macaluso's Dago-red. KING radio was torturing my ears with Henry Busse's "Wang, Wang Blues"–I didn't care, I had my music from within. I was planning my treat. I had rented the Fellowship Hall, which was a step up from the usual Oddfellows. I was surprised to find it had only cost $165. Hell, I'd walked away from the country club with more than that and I still had another check from Tacoma Screw before the happening. I was way ahead of the game. I'd hired a trio–piano, drums, and bass–just for the heavies, but ten friends had promised to come and jam. Some of the Ultra Club cats had volunteered to decorate and serve, I guess they just wanted to be there–over two thousand square feet of dance floor and only two couples–wow. I was still counting the musicians, like Scott with his valve trombone, Buz with his clarinet, Kenny with his cornet, Karry with her sweet French horn, when I must have fallen asleep.

Moon

Early the next morning I was rattled into consciousness by a very ugly phone. Abby was on the other end telling me Babs was leaving. "Babs was afraid to tell you. It's not her fault. It's her doctor." I was dead to the world, but I think I was following the stream. "Her father doesn't want her to go, either; but apparently her doctor has been planning this for weeks–six months with great doctors in a quiet sanitarium near Palermo. They have family there. A small price to pay to relieve a troubled mind–that's the argument they used on her father; he finally caved in. He's lost one already. He's scared to death for Babs."

In a trance I dialed Babs' number. Her father's male secretary answered, "She's being sent to Europe for health reasons," click! Trapped, I couldn't even speak to her. I called the Kid.

I was walking the garage, by the time he arrived I'd covered at least five miles. "You want to see her?" he asked. "I can get you in there."

We were about to leave when Abby called back. "I'm so glad I caught you, I don't want you to do something you'll regret, Moon," she said. Kid picked up the other line. "There are some things about Babs you've only seen hints of. You should know all the facts. First she might really need this help. No, I don't want to hide behind a *might*. I say she *does* need this help. I'm her best friend. I love her, too. She needs it! And second, what you don't know is her mom committed suicide. It was hushed so she could be buried in the Church. And third, something additionally tragic happened. Her father went into shock and temporarily couldn't or wouldn't identify the body. The authorities said a family member had to identify the remains–it's policy. The body had been in the City Waterway under the Eleventh Street Bridge for three days–you can imagine. A juvy detective, you guessed it, your friend Smithy, picked her up and forced her to make the identity. God, she was only twelve at the time! "Remember, Moon, when she got drunk that time and started talking about dead eyes and pus... One time she said to me, 'Am I crazy like my mother? Crazier, yes, I'm crazier!'"

I was sure I was going to vomit, couldn't move. Kid hung up his extension, grabbed my phone, and screamed, "Screw you, Abby!" into the receiver than threw it on the floor. "We're going to see her, Moon!" he said. I stood there confused. "Let's go get her!" he pleaded. I hesitated. He had my sleeve. I saw myself as a simple kid, getting in the great doctor's way; there was so much new information I still hadn't digested. I could harm her. What did I know of mental illness? She could follow her mother; it would be my fault.

I spun out of Kid's grasp, leaving him holding my empty jacket. "I can't, I can't!" I screamed as I ran away. Afterwards I slept for two days, consciousness was unbearable.

Stella

That fall I was doing graduate work at the University of Washington. I selected the new Tacoma Youth Center for my major project. My aging professor, I think he hated sociology by that time in his career, demanded that I spend five hours a week at the Center, and while there, that I never ask a direct question, that I never conduct an interview by any method, and that I answer every question put to me. "I don't give a damn if they ask who you slept with last night! I want no judgements, and no notes taken on site. Of course, I'll want copious notes from your dorm. I want only clauses—no complete sentences. Sentences beget judgements. And I don't want you to hand out advice, either. These people are to be your equals, your family, your friends."

"But, if I can't ask questions," I asked at last, "how am I to..."

"That my dear is the difference between a sociologist and a dunce!" he snapped. I hated the son of a bitch, but I knew he had the respect of his colleagues. He had spent ten years in the field before surrendering to academia. My first week at the Youth Center I did my best to act friendly, but got back only polite retreats. Luckily, I was able to help Dela, the club secretary, with some heavy typing. She could do about thirty words a minute, next to my 100. We became instant friends. She was the quiet artistic type, but when something excited her, she energized and lit up the room, and when it happened, you had the feeling: this is what we've all been waiting for–she was adorable! That unpredictability, shapely figure, June Christy hairstyle, and classy clothes made her a hit with the boys. She, however, seemed to pay little attention to any of them. In a few days she freely gave me more information than I could have garnered in weeks of interviews. When I had her complete confidence, she told me she was in love with Moon. He was tall, cute with a wild DA hairdo, as they called it, really it was just initials for 'duck's ass,' because that was exactly what it looked like in the back! She asked what I thought of him? "He's darling," I said, "but he's not my type."

I could see she was a little taken back. "Just who is your type, then?" she demanded.

I had been watching the one they called the Kid dance with a short, body beautiful, blond with hip length hair. Abby, I think they called her. It was a warm afternoon; I was warm, too. His sports coat and tie were hanging over a chair. His pink dress shirt, stretched tight at the biceps, had a wide rolled collar and French cuffs. His gray flannels were tailored to the hips, full in the knees, and pegged at the bottom. You could see his gluteus maximus–his buns, flexing as he shimmied, first with the right then with the left. His broad shoulders were well back; so the nearest part of his anatomy to hers was his scrotum. I had let myself slide down in my seat stretching my panties tight over my perineum. It felt good, and I squealed, "him!" pointing at the Kid.

"But, he's shorter than you, Stella," she laughed.

"I'll get shorter; just park my shoes under his bed and I'll be five feet tall if he wants," I said.

"I don't believe you, Stella! You're too much!" She

jumped up cackling. People began to notice; I grabbed her arm, pulling her back down.

"Just kidding, no pun intended." I said.

"You lie, you wicked punster, you meant every word of it!"

"I know," I answered, "isn't it wonderful?"

I was finally accepted at the Youth Center. I danced often with everyone, learning the routines was easy, ridding myself of the horsiness of excess size was the real problem. Moon and Kid were especially generous with their time. Teaching me to bop became their project. Lots of the boys, I'm certain, just danced with me for my big tits. I'd feel then press me, but I thought, oh well, what are breasts for anyway. I had gone there thinking Bing and Bob Crosby were the jazz brothers, and Patti Page was the Queen of Lyrics. Moon called me "the impoverished one." He taught me how to pick out a riff, which thrilled me. He also taught me the word was *hip* not *hep*, and that "BC" meant "before Christy."

Slow dancing with the Kid was my heaven. By slow I mean cheek to cheek, breast to breast, as opposed to jitter-bugging or bopping. That doesn't mean the movement was slow or that we stayed in one place, far from it. The jukebox had a soaring rendition of "Stella by Starlight," certainly the only thing on the box with strings. It required a totally different approach – classic, I guess you could call it. I don't know where he learned, who inspired him; I know he loved Gene Kelly, but only tolerated Fred Astaire. Whatever, he had the gift. His chest would hit me just under my breasts, lifting me, his right arm strongly around my waist, and his left arm almost straight. I felt as if I weighed 115 pounds. I was Cyd Charisse spinning, sweeping, and swooping in a seamless collage of moves. The dance floor was only twenty by twenty, but we'd swing through the furniture trebling its size and adding immense variety. To cool off I'd quickly pick "Again," by Doris Day.

He'd say," Oh, no, not 'Again,'" I'd laugh and crush my breasts into his chest and I'd feel him on my pelvis as we slowly rocked. I didn't know what little Miss Abby could do for him; but nothing, I'd tell myself to what I could!

"Again" proved to be prophetic, I knew nothing, no one would ever move me like that. I was forever indebted to those friends, to my family. In four and a half months I had learned to love music, dance, honesty, and more. So, when Dela came to me asking that I write a couple of chapters of my experiences with the boys, how could I not? She thought that with my training I might have some objectivity. Shit! I haven't an objective thought of either of them. And, when I think of the Kid I still say, "Steady, Stella!"

Kid

My wish list was complete; there was no more room for gifts under my tree. I had my family, not the one dealt me, but the one I'd selected. Moon and I, though similar in tastes, were opposites in most other things. He opened me up, made me laugh, and I knew I needed that. I had fake laughter in the past, now there was no need–it came rolling right over the top of me, honest and fulfilling. And Babs opened me to art. She designed these intricate, delicate dolls. I was in awe of them, afraid to touch them; so she threw one hard, right at my face. I had to catch it just to keep from getting hurt. "Art is alive you must live with it, not view it from afar," she said. And Babs kept Abby grounded. When Abby's little rich-girl nose would go off in space, Babs would say, "Now Abby, I'm not going to tell these nice boys you were masturbating last night." Abby would screech. Babs would continue, "But, I did see your bed shaking in that certain way!" With that kind of material constantly unfolding, there was no way you could take yourself too seriously. "Just get over yourself," was everyone's favorite line. I never thought of being in love with Abby. I had to be near her, but I had to be near Moon and Babs, too. I could imagine no other existence. I could sense a bit of smugness in my feelings towards Abby; she had the kind of presence that made everyone want her, and she was with me! She never gave me a second to worry, and she was pleased I was that way for her. Surpris-

ingly, Babs' father was the next closest person to our foursome. We spent a great deal of time in Babs' apartment; it
was centrally located, it was comfortable, and Mr. Arno made
us welcome. He'd personally wheel in that big silver cart
full of goodies from the pastry chef. When he wasn't visible,
Moon was sure there were sophisticated listening devices. I
didn't believe he was anything but what he seemed - one
great dad. When we were out of his sight, his presence was
felt in proxy–the Buick Roadmaster. Sure, I was nervous early
on, but I began to look at him as a friend. Babs' survival
framed Mr. Arno's existence; I'm certain he could sense we
were good for her. Moon would balk at this, but I think the
don began to look at us as family. That's why on that final
day I knew I could talk him out of sending her away. It's
tough to argue against an authority figure like her doctor.
The doctor made a pronouncement and the old man buckled. I could have asked what the doctor had done for her so
far? Did he personally know any of the new doctors that
would be treating her? Sicily could seem like the other side
of the moon for her. And I could have reminded him that
she'd be leaving everything she loved–her car, her apartment,
her school, her dad, her boyfriend, the rest of her friends,
heck even me. And not to mention, her dolls; how could you
separate Babs from her dolls? If her being was so fragile how
could she survive a loss like that? Who could say she hadn't
been maintaining? I had been close to her. I had seen inside,
I'm in want to say her soul; a glimpse of something I'd never
seen before–a vulnerability that could give the feeling that it
could plunge her and perhaps any bystander into an abyss,
but it hadn't, and she was still standing there, her chin jut-
ting out, saying "Hey world, I can take what ever you dish

out" No, Abby and Moon could have folded on Babs; I didn't have to. I could have gone around them, but to my ever-lasting shame in my own way I, too, collapsed. Indeed, with the foundation pulled from beneath her feet, the world she had challenged was free to crush her. I could have…I should have…

Moon

They sent her body back from New York. She never made it to Sicily with that wonderful sanitarium. Her father, the aunt, Abby, Kid and I, that was all they allowed inside the funeral chapel. A silver casket rested on six golden pillars, about three feet off the floor. It was centered in the small room, flanked by dozens of dolls, each with its own unique floral arrangement provided by Ghilarducci. There were no chairs. An old priest muttering some bothersome shit in Latin, stood next to the casket. I saw Mr. Arno wave him off. The priest, looking confused and hurt struggled to the door. The five of us, holding hands, kneeled about six feet away from the coffin. We hugged and cried. Then her father broke his grip with my hand and crawled on top of the casket, hugging it, holding it as if he could keep her there. At last he slipped down, lay on his back, crying. I tried to stop myself, but I had to see. I could not spend the rest of my life not knowing. I charged forward, ripped open the coffin. It was… I wanted to get in there with her. I felt the Kid's hand on my shoulder and we walked out in the Tacoma rain. A large crowd of Babs' schoolmates was at the door, crying. Abby was still at the foot of the coffin when I looked back. I never saw her again, and I didn't see much of the Kid; I heard he had left town. My wheels rolled to halt. I slept and wrote a lot of silly poetry, mostly stuff like:

The four of us had been one

Now, without one
There were none.

I cried often, I'd just look at the wall and break down.
I had to hide the dolls and the other gifts she'd given to me.
I was really worried about my manhood. One day, perhaps
a week after the Kid returned I charged myself up, hoping
he had come to terms with my weakness. I knew he had
thought I deserted her. I called him. We met at Don's Restaurant. Other than the Center, that was where we met Babs
and Abby downtown. There was a full-length mirror facing
the counter. Rae, our favorite waitress, was struggling to take
our order. We both started crying. Rae finally walked off in
embarrassment. I started to gain control after that; if the Kid
could still cry for her; so could I, by god! It was okay.

There were chicks I liked to be with, but as compan-
ions only. Verna was one, but she'd get after me. Dela was
especially good for me; we'd talk and talk, and she didn't
pry into the cracks. Girls were my best friends and unlike
cats they were always there; and with the exception of Verna,
always kept the distance I'd imposed on them. But, Mary
Lee was one I craved, if I could only talk to her...

Moon

After the Kid came back from his island, he started spreading his wings. The Youth Center was almost forgotten. He went to work at Bennies'–the hippest clothing store in town, anywhere maybe. He always had a wardrobe. Hell, he wore a suit or sports coat to school everyday. No one in town dared something like that. They wore pegged denims or dirty white cords, topped with a Lord Jeff lamb's wool sweater, maybe cashmere for one in a hundred. For openers Kid had four suits, all cool one-button sacs. Then he had two sports coats, plus a navy blue yacht club blazer. With a half dozen Mr. B dress shirts, an equal number of Hartog jerseys, and a couple of Hampton sport shirts, he could vary it at will. But the nerve of the cat, only teachers wore suits to school. Every morning the girls used to sneak down the hall and peak into his homeroom just to be first to report what he was wearing that day. He could have any of them, but like me he wasn't into relationships these days.

One day Kid came to me with an unbelievable proposition–Mr. Arno wanted me to have the phaeton. "Why would he?" I asked.

"It's a symbol of the loss of both Barbara and Babs," Kid began slowly, "He can't stand seeing it around; at the same time, he can't tolerate selling it to a stranger. The way I see it, you were the only logical choice. You should take it, do you want to see his secretary driving it?"

Frankly, I was afraid of the thing, Barbara Arno who had been a painter, and wealthy in her own right, participated in its design. It was begun in 1941 by the renown coachbuilders, Bohmann & Schwartz, and obediently set aside during the war. But after struggling three years with gross war vehicles, the employees found it a labor of love and logged all their shop time on the phaeton. It was delivered on January 2, 1946 in a state of perfection. It had never required maintenance beyond the obligatory lube and oil change. I wasn't worried what a punk kid would look like driving that machine; I'd already tried that one on and it was a fit. What scared the hell out of me was what Babs had told me–for two years after her mom had died she had used the car as a secret crying place. She'd shown me the stains on the white leather. My head continued saying, "No way, don't you even think about accepting it." But I dreamed of sitting on the same seat that she had, then I thought of the secretary sitting there, so I said okay. One day it showed up in my driveway. I stood there waffling. What had I done? But I knew I couldn't just send it back.

The key and the title were in the mail drop. I drove it around–parking it at Bennies', Don's, Jack's Pool Hall, the Youth Center. I'd stand back and watch people look at it. I loved the envious looks when I opened the door, but I knew it wasn't to be kept. It took me a step backwards in my recovery; it was becoming my crying place, too. One day the Kid was watching me park it. I leaned out the window, "Let's torch it!" I said.

"I'm for it," he came back instantly. He had been reading me right, again. He said later, he was afraid I might purposely drive into a train or off a bridge. The car was uninsured, I foresaw no legal hassles, so that afternoon I reported it stolen, and that same evening we drove it to an old deserted mill at Old Town. It had a very long pier that was already a couple of inches under water at the out board end. I placed the four little dolls–Babs and me up front, Abby and Kid in the back; and lit the gas Kid and I had splashed. We hustled up to a prominent knoll about 150 yards up the long hill, and watched it burn. I don't know what the Kid was thinking; I felt an extreme sense of loss; I knew I would never again possess anything of that value, and I did love it, but at the same time I felt an even larger sense of release.

People started to gather, watching. The first was a drunk. I looked at him. He was about 6'3" with curly red hair. A little pot folded over his belt; he was about forty-five. Staggering, fighting to hold his position on the knoll, "Who torched her?" he asked. I didn't answer. "Who burned her!" he demanded.

"I saw the guy run away," I answered. "Say, what's your name anyway?"

"Al," he answered.

"Well, Al, he was a tall guy, maybe 6' 3," red hair, kind of curly, old clothes." I started to say about forty-five, but my conscience caught me and I said he was an old guy, with a limp. I heard him repeat it to some other people on the knoll, then to a couple farther down the hill. By morning everyone would know who did it; the Tacoma rumor press was stronger than the *News Tribune* ever hoped to be. We walked to my place in the Proctor district, about three miles, mostly up hill. We stopped from time to time to watch. Finally, the pier buckled, and we heard a giant hiss as the Cadillac phaeton was swallowed by Puget Sound. It proved to be good decision–one more funeral, one more chance to grieve.

Kid

At Babs' funeral I felt I was in a siege, surrounded by the enemies that had murdered my friend. I held their hands, coddled them, and despised them, and yet only a few days earlier I would have killed for them. And what of the arch enemy, Smithy? He had started the events that had led to this. As I saw it now, he was hardly guiltier than the rest. Still, it would have been easy to take vengeance on him. I knew for the first time in my life, I wanted to hurt someone; and if I stayed around, it was going to be Smithy. Instead, I took one of the little flatties, my last pint of Old Rocking Chair, some canned goods, hard rolls, and coffee; then sailed through the Narrows, under the big bridge, and west to Cutts' Island. After a few days the supplies ran out. It was late winter, and it felt good to be hungry, cold, and in near shock. By the end of the week I realized I was the one I wanted to hurt, and I was doing a good job of it. I returned to town, planning to leave Tacoma and try my luck in sunny California.

My plans, however, were thwarted by my old friend Bennie who offered me a job in my favorite clothing store. It wasn't out of the blue, he'd been looking for me for two weeks. He knew about Babs, she had been in the store with Moon and me, but he seemed to know everything, and you could tell he cared. I took the job. I thought I was finished with school, with so many unexcused absences I couldn't personally dare ask Lincoln to take me back. So, Bennie called

Lincoln for me, of course they politely refused him, but then he called a friend of his at Stadium and I was in, no questions asked.

I was feeling better than I had any right to feel. Death had taken one of my best friends; in the process I had lost the chick I'd spent every free hour with for the best part of a year. I don't know what happened between Abby and me, but with Babs gone I couldn't think of being with her. The wonder machine we'd enjoyed had four wheels it couldn't work with three. I could not look at her.

I had difficulty even looking at Moon at first–the anguish. Also, that same vulnerability I had previously seen only in Babs, now seemed to permeate Moon. I was worried about him. When I didn't see him around, I'd have to go find him. Usually, he'd be in the pool hall with Whitey.

Then out of the blue Mr. Arno's secretary called offering Moon the phaeton. To my surprise, Moon accepted. Then one night Moon and I walked away from its sizzling remains down in Old Town. The following week the Youth Center closed. The papers reported charges that the Reverend Powers was selling dope to the cats. I hadn't been there lately because Smithy had taken residence, but I couldn't help thinking that he'd stashed the dope. In three years, I'd seen one can of Rainier there. Again, I saw that Tacoma devoured its saints faster than its villains.

Moon's dream was to open a coffeehouse and he'd always loved that USO nickelodeon; so I dug into my cigar box, put the bill of sale in his hand, and said, "It's yours, Bra." But when Moon and three of his musician friends went to retrieve it, they were stopped by Smithy who was called by the new tenant. Moon handed Smithy's partner the bill of sale; He read it; then handed it to Smithy. "This don't mean shit!" he scoffed. "As soon as it was placed in the Center it became City property!"

"I guess we'll have to see what the judge says," Moon argued.

"Don't give me none of your shit; you little punk; I'm the judge here!" Now, Moon never initiated a fight in his life. He used to brag, "I've been in three fights in my life, and I've lost four of them." But something in him, perhaps it was Babs, I'd like to think so, made him lift the back of his hand and slap Smithy, a real zinger, I'm told. But that was exactly what Smithy wanted, he pounded Moon, and held him, keeping him from falling, so he could maneuver him to go down that flight and a half of stairs.

"Man injured while resisting arrest," that's what the *News Tribune* said. I knew I was supposed to do something, cats expected it, I expected it. I knew Smithy would be looking over his shoulder, too; but I also knew my life would be over as I had known it. Anything that happened to him would have my signature on it. At best I'd be a fugitive, but more probable, I'd be in jail, and if that happened, Smithy would still be the winner. I tried to see Moon in the County Hospital, but no one could get in. Later, when he was well enough, I visited him at Western Washington Mental Hospital at Steilacoom. They said he was being detained for observation, pending criminal charges, but my boss knew the doctors, so they let me see him. I first saw him from a distance lying across a chaise lounge in the middle of a big ward. He didn't look bad, except his right leg was in a full cast.

"Hey," I said, "let me be the first to autograph your cast." His gray eyes looked up at me trying to distinguish me. He gave up after a few seconds. I wrote, "The Kid," on his cast, which he seemed to decipher. He looked again at me, really seeing me this time.

"I never got to do my treat," his voice, weak and breaking. I struggled to find words. "I never got to do my treat," he repeated.

I exploded, running for several miles after I hit the hospital gates. I had to find Smithy and beat him to death, nothing else would do! I planned how it would work, I'd say this is for Babs and beat the left side of his face in; then I'd revive him and say this is for Moon and smash the right side. It had to be his face; he had to see it, and he had to know it was me. I walked back to town, probably another seven or eight miles. I went to Browne's for coffee, Bennie, my boss, was there. He stopped sweet-talking the new waitress, when he saw my disheveled look, "You found out, huh?"

"Yeah, I guess I did," I answered.

"I stuck around, hoping to catch you. I know your sense of obligation to Moon so I talked to Captain Amundsen. He owes me dough. He said they were going to send Moon to the State Pen at Monroe, but the don spoke for him, imagine that? The captain said he never heard of that, neither have I. Look, Kid, sending him to Western was the best thing that could have happened, you'll see. They will have to let him go as soon as they determine he's all right. You listen to Bennie, he'll be fine. It will be like momentary insanity. I know, I served on the board; the docs there never let a guy like Moon go to prison."

I told him what I had seen. He assured me Moon was just doped up. "They do that," he said, "to all the new inmates so they won't cause trouble. What luck, though, getting Arno in his corner; he must really care for Moon. Moon doesn't need you and me anymore. He'll be out in six weeks, two months at the most!"

Kid

I went to my new pad, stumbled over a box of new
tile, and fell in to a hot shower. I could hear the "Bob
Summerise Show" on KTAC. His first hour was called "The
Cool Breeze" and was all improvisational stuff; then for the
rest of the evening he switched to rhythm and blues with a
little Basie, Ellington and Kenton thrown in for relief. Bob
was the first Negro disc jockey in the area, and we became
friends when I helped him negotiate an advertising deal with
my boss. Bennie was Tacoma's icebreaker. When he hired
me everyone thought he was out of his mind, but he had
known me for years. He said he was just waiting for me to
grow up because he had watched me sell since I was seven.
Sure, it was just newspapers and shoeshines, but it still represented ten years of closing experience. Within a few weeks
I was outselling everyone else two to one. Also, I was a draw-
ing card; wannabes would want the Kid to select a suit or a
sports coat for them. It gave them talking power. Then, of
course the girls would come by and have me pick something
for their dad or their boyfriend. Bennie used to laugh, "You
don't have to sell anything, just keep those little dumplings
coming in and you'll have a job for life!"

A few days after I visited Moon, this beautiful brunette came in. Another salesman met her at the door, but she
asked if I could help her. Usually when a girl asked for me
she had a girlfriend or two with her, protection I guess, but

this one was alone. She wore an expensive black wool gabardine suit, a matador hat, Joyce pumps, and a delicate lavender blouse. "I'd like a shirt for my dad's birthday," she said. I showed her an Arrow and a Hathaway. "No," she turned in the stylish way a model would, "I'd like something more hip, like these," pointing to a Hampton dog-eared collar and a Mr. B high-rolled collar shirt.

"Look," I pressed her for eye contact which she slowly conceded, unless your father is a jazz musician, he's not..."

"I know," she interrupted, "it's really for a boyfriend, well he's not...Now, I am embarrassed!" She lowered her eyes. "I didn't want you to think I had a boyfriend."

"I am flattered," I bowed. "Why don't we go some quiet place and have a cup of coffee and talk about this?" I presented my arm, "Mademoiselle?" I asked. She put her hand inside my elbow, and we walked across the street to Browne's Star Grill. Dick Browne's eyebrows raised as we entered, and without asking he seated us in my favorite corner booth. Now that I had her there, I didn't know where to begin. Her face was dazzling me, and the way Dickie kept looking back I guess it was dazzling him, too. I reached across the table, taking her hand as a chill raced through my body. I looked into her eyes, "You are the most adorable creature I've ever seen."

She blushed, but instantly gained composure, "Is that all? I thought you were going to read my palm," she kidded.

"I was," I confessed, "but my tactile system lit up then I went tilt." We laughed and I released her hand, but she slipped it under mine and with her other hand opened my fingers.

"Then I'll read yours." she began. Beginning with my

fingertips, she slowly traced each finger to my lifeline base. "You," she began slowly, "are going to meet a dark haired girl, 5' 3", blue eyes, a few tiny, tiny freckles on her nose; and you're going to fall madly in love with her."

"You do believe in taking charge, don't you?" I pulled my hand away.

She reached over and retrieved my hand, "This chick has been waiting two years for you to notice her. She's done everything, but pull your coat, and you've totally ignored her. And, now that you've transferred to Stadium she never gets to see you!"

It can't be I thought. This girl's from Lincoln? She looks too old for high school. Besides, how could I have missed her? The clothes, I thought. My mind's eye put her in a cashmere sweater and a pegged skirt and went searching Lincoln's halls for her likeness. Then I caught her. I called up a short, very short blond chick, and a tall freckled face doll with hip length light brown hair; and this energetic brunette right in the middle. "I've got you fixed," I said, "you're Star."

"It took you long enough," she pouted.

"And," I continued, "I know your tall girlfriend, Beverly. She's my..."

"Yes, Bev," she stopped me, "has told me every word you have ever uttered to her."

I relaxed and leaned my head against the booth, "How is it that I deserve such attention, Star?"

"How is it that Star deserves such lack of attention?" she demanded.

I stewed on that one a bit while watching Dickie go to the jukebox and select a Stan Getz medley. He knew how to tease me. The tunes I knew would be on my check. I reached over and took her hand again, kissing it. I saw a tear come from the corner of her eye, roll down her cheek, and disappear down her neck. "The answer is easy, you deserve more, much more than me. I have too many strings. Hell, not strings–ropes, cables, chains. I don't want to sound melodramatic, but I can't count on a future right now."

"Are you still in love with Abby?" she asked.

"No, I still love the idea of Abby, but I'm not sure I was ever in love with her. Anyway, it's over, out of service, defunct!" I said.

"Such finality, I hope you never feel that way about me."

"That's just it, I can never be involved with anyone until I can break out of this." I answered.

"It's about Moon, isn't it?" she asked.

"How do you know so much?"

"I know all about Moon, I used to watch the two of you showboating at the Oddfellows and the Fellowship. I know you talked him into leaving home, that's common knowledge, and like everyone in town, I know about Moon, you, and that cop. People are betting you'll get into it with him. You think you're responsible for Moon."

"No, I know I'm not responsible in the strict sense, but he's my brother and I must keep things right." Changing the subject, "Hey, how about that boyfriend's shirt?"

"What size do *you* wear?" she laughed. "Actually, I've two boyfriends but they are just platonic."

"Well, I'll be your third platonic boyfriend for awhile, okay?"

My check said: Stan Getz, $1.00. I guess it was fair enough, he didn't charge for the coffee. We met for our *pla-*

tonic lunch every Saturday thereafter; she'd be on her way to her modeling class, so she'd be impeccably dressed, I refused to give details at the store; it would have spoiled it for them had they known she was only a junior in high school. They'd say, "Here comes that mystery woman!" And my senses would desert me.

Stella

I saw quite a bit of Moon after they committed him to Western because I did four hours a week there as part of my public health program. His leg was healing fine, but his head was slow to mend. His doctor, old reliable Reilly, said he was typical of a jailhouse case. The surgery on the leg was satisfactory, but he had received no nursing care. "They had detected the head injury, but had missed some pretty severe upper abdominal trauma. When he arrived I was looking at both epigastria and mental shock, and beyond that, vermin–lice everywhere!"

He had, obviously, done a lot for Moon. I first came away thinking they were giving him excellent care, but then they started giving him shock treatment for Christ's sake! I asked Moon about the effects. He said the pain was so massive and the fear of death so complete, it appeared to the docs that it worked, because your fortitude would collapse, bringing you into a state of total abeyance. I saw it as temporarily swapping depression for acute anxiety–one evil for another. What was the gain?

One thing that comforted me about Moon was his predictability; he was uni-polar. His mood shifts were always to the depressed side–situational, that's what the books call it. You could expect it, almost call it normal after a catastrophic loss and major injuries. What were his symptoms: lack of enthusiasm, sleep disturbance, dejection. Hell, it didn't take an Adler, Jung, or a Freud to know that was simple depression. Give him an antidepressant and kick his ass out. Of course, I couldn't tell Reilly any of this. He'd have thrown me out, I hate psychiatrists, anyway, the pompous assholes.

The Kid called me, wanting me to go with him to Mr. Arno's. The don had asked for the meeting. I jumped at the chance; here was a player I hadn't met. He and Moon shared the same syndrome; they had both lost everything. The empty envelope was the on the doorstep with a big red stamp saying "return to sender." Mr. Arno had lost what had apparently been the love of his life and then the daughter of that love who, by all accounts was devoted to him. What could keep someone like that going after such losses? Moon's mother had died in the delivery room; his dad, blaming Moon, withholds his love, but Moon, pulling himself up by his own shoestrings, puts together a love, a life, and a family, and then loses it all in a matter of a few days. My prayer is that his depression will be self-limiting, run its course, then exit. And, again he'll pull himself up by those same shoestrings. As to Mr. Arno, he must have a pair of stout laces, indeed.

An elderly housekeeper opened the door to the apartment and led us down a long hall to a large office. The secretary nervously picked up his steno tablet, pressed it to his ribs, and prissied out. (See? I'm not judgmental.) Mr. Arno, very graciously, had coffee, tea, and pastries prepared on a large silver serving cart. A male server appeared, served us, then quickly exited. The don, a handsome man with salt and pepper hair, had deep wrinkles but sparse.

He spoke slowly, "I've some rather good news. The juvenile detective, one sergeant Smithington Tennant, has been reprimanded. Highly unusual for the T.P.D., but appropriate, nonetheless. He'll not receive his expected lieutenant's bars," a slight smile came to his lips. "Further, he is back in uniform and assigned to a squad car–a real come down, I should think!" His look was one of self-satisfaction and I thought he was going to come right out and laugh, but instead he assumed an inscrutable stare while his words flowed in a controlled monotone. "They decided he lacks the sensitivity to deal with youths." He paused, reviving himself, "Now, what can you tell me about Moon's condition? I'm disinclined to trust doctors these days."

Both Kid and I thought it best that Moon be released as soon as possible; the risks, we thought, were greater on the inside. "I couldn't agree more," he said. Then he presented a program he had negotiated which we in turn, were to present to Moon. It was simple; Moon had to agree to a year's therapy with a private psychiatrist, for which Mr. Arno would pick up the tab. We could choose the shrink, Moon could choose; but Dr. Reilly would also have to approve of him. What was most pleasing, after that year no matter what anyone thought, Moon was entitled to an unconditional release.

As we were leaving Mr. Arno said to the Kid, "Congratulations on your final solution to the phaeton, I approve!" He resumed his inscrutable stare as he walked us to the door, but at the last moment he turned and hugged Kid. It seemed incongruous but Kid appeared comfortable with it.

"What did he mean, *he approved?*" I snapped when we were outside. I had an idea what had happened, but I couldn't believe it.

"He means," he answered, "he liked the Viking funeral. I couldn't guess how he'd feel; it's good he wanted it, too."

He explained the torching as I was opening the door to my beater Plymouth. I was at first appalled, but when he elaborated, I liked it, too. He also filled me in on his history, as a boxer, street fighter, and his relationship with Abby and Babs. It was spooky, Babs was his chosen sister; people just didn't run around choosing sisters; I wondered if he hadn't loved her, too.

Perhaps, I was too narrow, nothing in my training prepared me for this. At least I was feeling a little more objective towards him. Stella was hopefully getting over herself. I wasn't always thinking of him in relation to my body. That was always the talk I was giving myself, "God-damnit, Stella get over yourself!" I knew it was just a crush. That's where you love someone that's out of reach, and that someone doesn't love you back. I knew I had no right to him, the disparity in size and age alone; still, there was that quality about him that made me all hot and runny. Without the slightest hint of smugness he carried himself like he could handle anything that came along, and he didn't just love music, dance, literature, and art–he lived it! You could feel it in him. That filled my dance card, right there.

It was decided that I would drive Moon home from the hospital. I was familiar with the routine; so I could make it more comfortable for him. They'd taken him off drugs so I was getting my first real look at him. Except for being a little shaky he seamed in perfect control. Using our standard interview method, I flipped him a group of questions, which he fielded easily. Finally he said, "You sound like Dr. Reilly." I shut up.

My worry was Sergeant Tennant–Smithy. I'd first met him at the Center that fall. Talk about making your flesh crawl! He tried to ingratiate himself, and hinted I should tell him what I learned. I told him I didn't do police work. He shunned me after that which was okay by me. But, now I couldn't help thinking, he'd be even more dangerous. The sting of his demotion and the loss of his cushy nine to five job had to fire his anger. Besides, now his shift coincided with the dangerous night hours on the street. He knew all the hangouts; he'd be there, the malevolent son of a bitch.

When we opened Moon's door, a welcoming party was in progress. Lionel Hampton's "Flying Home" was coming from the big red, white and blue box in the corner. Moon was home and flying, so I aimed for a quick exit, but before I got to the car the Kid caught my arm.

"Come on back, we've got some celebrating to do!" I kicked off my heels and we slid together as Ben Webster's lyrical sax pumped out "I got it bad and that ain't good." Kid had never let me lead, but I'm sure I was leading when we hit the bedroom door. So much for good intentions! I won't pretend; he could have come at me with a tallywacker the size of a matchstick; it would have sufficed. But he didn't and it wasn't. It had been a heavy grind, and the denouement had been a long time coming. Call it gratuitous sex, call it what you like; but I went over the top. I was lighter than air. His appendage was everywhere I wanted it to be–between my breast, in my neck, in my mouth, in my vagina. His arms were like steel parallel bars; I could hang on indefinitely, allowing me to glide and shimmy, creating a sweet erotic dance. I was certain no one had ever experienced anything like that before nor would anyone ever again. *Again?*

There goes that song "Again." Ah, shit, a pun on a *pun;* God will never forgive me now!

Moon

I started to get on with my lot. I gave up my job at the Screw Products. I had an idea of opening a coffeehouse, the first one in Tacoma. I had a spot on St. Helens, sizeable, but with cheap rent. I had the Kid's big nickelodeon; I had a dozen musicians who were committed to fill in gigs for tips; and I had poets–there were more repressed beatnik poets in Tacoma than Douglas firs. How could I miss?

Then I got nailed on that thing with Smithy. I'm still not clear on the incident. Oh, I know what happened, plenty of people have filled me in on that; it's the *why* I can't fix. I thought I was immune to that sort of a trap at this stage in my life. Four of us were trying to carry the jukebox. It had an awkward shape, and it must have weighed over 400 pounds. We got as far as the stairs. Buz went to get the handtruck. It was warm. Dick and Bernie were standing there sweating. I was sweating in two ways: one, I was perspiring, sweat was running into my eyes and down my nose; and two, I was beset with anxiety as to how I was going to get that monster down that long, long stair case. Then Smithy came bounding up the stairs, taking them in pairs.

I could see he wanted to bite someone's ass off. His body language said, "Get out of my way, punk!" Maybe it was just that, the insult. But I was also remembering his part in Babs' death. So, to irk him I gave the bill of sale to his partner. The next thing I knew his Juicyfruit breath was in my face, and he was thumping me in the chest with those big round fingers of his. I could lay the slap off to stimulus/response–Pavlov's dog in action; but I remember thinking this evil fuck, fucks with people, even my Babs! I woke once at the foot of the stairs as they were putting me in the stretcher; then the fog rolled over me. When I woke again, my head was throbbing, my gut hurt, and my leg was encased in a full cast. The orderly saw I was conscious, I couldn't have moved had I wanted; but he freaked, and the next thing I knew I was in a cart on my way to a hospital cell. I can only believe they had lost me. I had fallen through their system. After the cart stopped moving, I started vomiting. No one came. It dried on my neck, plugged my nose; and still no one came. I could see water on the table, but it was just out of reach. I went out again, for how long, I don't know; but when I woke, the bed was wet, and I had had at least one bowel movement–shit everywhere, on my hands and in my nose, where I'd tried to pick some of the barf out of the air passage. But worse, I was burning up and tried for that water again, this time falling out of the cart. I could see the shiny cement floor coming at my face, but the lights went out again. When I woke again I was at Steilacoom, Washington, the "home of the loony-tunes," as Stella would say.

You know what happened to me there; I read what Stella said, and that was pretty much it except for the part about Babs' death. You see I'd never known how she did it. I could have asked. They'd have told me. But I didn't, and so it began: I'd imagine four scenarios–she took sleeping pills, she took rat poison, she stepped in front of a taxi, she used a little pearl handled revolver. They took on chaotic forms–falls, fits, seizures, bleeding bones, puss oozing from tissue.

It was depriving me of my humanity. I had lost all quality of life. They played over and over in my mind's eye. The details were so specific; they'd come at me until I was nauseated and would vomit.

Of course I told Doc Reilly, and one day he said, "You need wonder no more. I spoke to her father and aunt; I can give you the whole business, if you like?"

"Please, please," I said.

He read from his notes. "She slipped from her aunt when they arrived at La Gaurdia, and took a room in a small hotel nearby." He paused, "Now, Moon, I've got to be exact, to give it to you exact, you understand."

"Yes, of course," I said." Please, go on."

"She poured a glass of white zinfandel, drank most of it, set the glass on the nightstand, then filled it again, and then slipped into a hot bath tub. She drank half the wine, set it on the floor next to the tub, and then slit both wrists with a Gillette double edge blade." He paused, looking at me, not reading. "They think she went to sleep, because when they found her, her eyes were closed, and they described a slight smile on her face. She left a twelve word note." He was reading again:

'Bye, Papa,
I love you, my Moonbeam
I can't help myself.
Babs

He handed me a copy. I'm certain that's what got me out of there. It gave me, for then, a complete visualization. That's what I live by–see it all, put it in its place. The bad scenes stopped coming.

My new shrink has proved helpful, too. He loves his tunes, mostly classical, but he does collect early blues artists like Bessie Smith. He's one of those people that believes art has to be old to be good. That's okay, but it's not me. But he's cool, I can say anything I want to him, and ask him anything, as well. He always gives me his honest answer, and he's the first doc to tell me his answer may be all bullshit. He thinks I should get back into my saxophone; he made me play it for him, and get this–he thinks I'm good! I'm going to pick up a class at College of Puget Sound.

Stella

I was working four days a week for Public Health, and the staff had dumped every loony on me; so I didn't see anyone for quite awhile. And I still had my eye on that PHD; so the rest of the time found me driving to the University of Washington in Seattle. It was a period of hard work, but also of satisfaction as I felt I was finally accomplishing something in my field. And I was actually getting comfortable with myself. My dancing experience had gone a long way towards making me comfortable with my body. I had never been fat, just big, bigger than I wanted to be. When I was thirteen I went through a bout with anorexia nervosa. My mother sent me to a psychiatrist. I was 5' 10" and had dieted to 109 pounds, but there was still enough flesh for some reasonable sized breasts. The old doctor took off my bra and fondled them. Oh, he pretended to be all scientific, but I could see he was getting all funny. I told my certifiable mother about him. She said, "Of all the luck! Did you screw him? I've been after that man for years!" No wonder I'm what I am, all the Knudsen women are a quarter turn out, one more little squeeze and we'd all be in straight jackets.

I bumped into Vic Marzano one night. Vic had been a Soc major when I started C.P.S. I didn't even know what sociology was then. Vic, big man on campus, showed me around, but it always ended in the back seat of his Chevy. How many ways could an eighteen year old freshman tell a twenty-one year old junior *no*? I tried them all, then one night I couldn't think of any. He dropped me right after that. I guess he couldn't stand success, and I knew I couldn't stand failure. I saw him only once shortly after, I think I spit on him, I'm not sure. There are degrees of hatred...but never mind that.

Anyhow, I almost collided with him coming out of the Music Box Theater. He was in a policeman's uniform. I remember he had dropped out of school, but I had never known why. I let him take me to coffee at the Red Rooster Cafe next to the Turf Smoke Shop. Don's or Lanes' would have been closer, but I didn't want to be seen in either of these with a fuzz. He told me a tale of woe about his demise in school: he had run out of funds, he was failing Statistics, his head was in a mess, and he didn't know what to do about Stella. So he just ran, ran from everything.

He said he came back to school to explain to me, but I wasn't having any. He also said he called me several weeks after he joined the Force, but I had my mother hang up; that I did remember, but I wasn't about to swallow six years in one gulp.

He told me he was working the youth beat–Ninth Street from "A" to Market. His sociology had gotten him the assignment. "They wanted someone with sensitivity, that was the department's watchword these days. I love this work; it's not all deadbeats like I had on lower Pacific and Commerce. And, my soc work does come in handy; sometimes I can actually help some cats rather than arrest them." I, of course, was pleased by what he was saying, as these were my Youth Center kids. On his beat, which included the Center, there were nine restaurants and one deli, and five were hangouts for various groups. They were all cats. They wore the costume–a brushed back DA hairdo, pegged pants, and an extra long suit coat. They could have long gold pocket chains, suede shoes, a wrap around overcoat, but if they had the do, the pegs and the coat, they were cats.

The cats had a common enemy–the serviceman; so they rarely fought each other. Further, the soldiers or "doggies" as they called them were blamed for nearly everything. A juvenile is caught with a fifth of booze; the cop says, "Where'd you get it, kid?" From a doggie, comes the answer. A window is kicked out, the cop says, "All right, who did it?" The cat answers, "It was that very doggie just going around that corner." There was justification for this animosity. A carload of soldiers would see a cat alone on a corner, scream "meeow" out the window and if no reinforcements came, they'd jump out and stomp him. The Kid described it as a side show. When he was a sophomore, they'd plant him on Ninth and Pacific. The gang would hide in the Reviera Theater. When a car full of doggies would stop to whale him, twenty cats would pour out and stomp them. I asked if it ever happened that they didn't show up in time?

"Hell, yes," he said, "The first doggie out was always a gift because while he was dealing with the door, I could deal with him. But, the others would soon be behind you; you had to be able to hit or kick backwards; when you could do that effectively you could survive the street. I told this to Vic and he said the same show was still playing at the Reviera. He said the MPs had recently intercepted a convoy, mostly military vehicles, with weapons enough to wipe out half of Tacoma.

"We don't mind the little fights, it's the big stuff like

that we've got to stop. Still, there will come the day..." I agreed. I told him I was still friends with the young people from the Youth Center, and that I was working with a number of others through my job with Public Health. We compared other notes and surprisingly, we had a lot of common causes.

Moon

You probably know I opened my coffeehouse–the House of Moon. Babs came up with that name when we first talked about it last Christmas. It's worked out about as I expected; I'm not doing the business I want, but it will come. My hours are 6 p.m. 'til midnight, so I can handle it myself, but just barely. Sweet Dela has been helping out on weekends. I've developed a mean espresso, too. I buy high quality green beans, then oven roast them 'til they are almost black. Like whisky, man it's got a kick. A legal drug, that's what it is! People love it. I usually start them out with cream and sugar; and soon they are taking it black. The entertainment has been a gas!

The poetry has been an unexpected treat, these beat cats pour out words like notes coming out of Diz's kinky trumpet. Of course, some of the stuff's pretty bad, but that just adds to the fun. "Get the hook!" That's what's most often heard around here. The musicians have been great; their tips have been few and far between, but they keep coming. Bernie does some great improvisational accompaniment to the poetry; his bass seems to really lend itself to that. When no one shows, I take my tenor and swing a little–a cool California style. They seem to like it. Friends are starting to show up. Whitey was by the other day and helped me open. Stella and her new beau came by the other night. Wow, she's looking good! Friday, Kid came by with his boss, Bennie. Kid told me about his new chick; he said he hadn't really dated her yet, but I could see her in his eyes! That brought up Abby. He said he runs into her from time to time, usually with that irritating rich boy, Willie Hogan. They look embarrassingly at each other, never speak, and just move on. Man, help me understand that, when I do, I might know something! Naw, I'll never know, shit.

I see Smithy in an unmarked squad car; looks like he still thinks he's a juvy. He hounds the spots where the kids hang out. Listen to me use that word *kids* like I was an old man or something. I guess I've crossed, I don't feel like a kid anymore, that act is closed, it's time to catch the next show, I'm almost twenty. Hold that curtain, here I come! Speaking of shows, I am involved in what they call the "Show of Shows," really it's just an overdone jam session. It has the reputation as having the hippest sounds in the Northwest, everyone's there. It's out of town a ways at Stanley's After Hours Club. Dela drives me, she's the tower I lean on, lately. The place swings from one to four; I don't know how she makes it to work the next morning, but she never complains. I've learned to do some really fast stuff like Bird. I read this piece about Miles Davis, where he almost quit Bird every night because he just couldn't keep up. If the great Miles could feel that way, I didn't have to worry about my similar feeling. "Fly Bird, I'll still catch you," I'd whisper to myself. I started playing along with Dizzy and Bird's record and I *was* catching!

Dela gets my audience going; she's the world's greatest claque. I wish I wanted her the way I wanted Babs. She's wonderful, and artistic like Babs. I wish... I do wish it so. She says, "It's okay, Moon, I just want to be with you." But I know it's not okay. Fucked, if it's okay! When you only have one life to live, you shouldn't have to live it with someone who is only half there for you. Fucked, if it's okay!

Stella

I met Vic at the Music Box Theater, a wonderful old converted vaudeville house with exotic chandeliers, opulent fixtures, ornate ceilings, and wonderful Axminster carpet. We watched *Viva Zapata* and cried as Marlon Brando died in storm of bullets. We had coffee with the movie crowd at Lanes.

After, he drove me home in his new, red Oldsmobile 88. I saw him often after that. He is always on his good behavior and I am able to pick the places. The first place I wanted to go was the House of Moon. The coffeehouse was rustic, but interesting–some might call it funky–sawdust floors, a long counter, small malt shop tables, with old fashioned wooden pony kegs to sit on. Oh, yes, and over the mirror, behind the counter, was a sizeable sign, "No smoking, not even cigarettes." When we arrived an imitation Carl Sandburg, his hair all a mess, was *Chicagoizing* Tacoma.

Your sulfuric smelters
Your acrid pulp mills
Your semibastionous brothels

and all that ruckus. After, Moon picked up his sax and soothed his way through "Early Autumn." There's something very satisfying about a solitary horn working its way through a piece like that. I wondered why Moon had taken such pains to disparage his musical ability. Even I could recognize this was a talent. On our way out, Moon was busy making a whipped espresso for another customer, but I stopped to introduce Vic anyway.

After that we visited the Bluenote Ballroom. I'd heard it was a sensation, but was afraid to go there alone; even though I knew the Kid would be there. It turned out, I needn't have been. He was working the door, and pulled us away from the ticket booth, stamped our hands, kissed mine, and ushered us inside. They were featuring an imported group from Kansas City, and the place swung! It was a very old building with unusual maple floors that trembled with the beat, increasing the sensation. The crowd was a pretty even mixture of colors, and Vic was clearly outside his experience, but I showed him some steps he could easily do, and he started having fun. Then a group of plainclothesmen appeared. "Ah, jeez," Vic said, turning red, "the fucking Vice Squad!"

Lieutenant Richey, a very large red haired man with thick features and pink skin, was stopping all mixed couples and asking for I.D. Then two of his officers would split them, leading them in opposite directions drilling them. "That's Gestapo tactics, and it's illegal every place but Tacoma!" Vic said in disgust.

I laughed trying to get him back to the fun mode, "Well, let's get your black ass out of here, before they notice this *wop* with the fine flaxen haired lass he's accompanying." The Kid stopped us on the way out.

"Richey chase you out, too?" he asked. "You just witnessed the last vestige of the 19th Century. And get this," Kid continued, "he once arrested a friend of mine. He's twenty-seven years old, his fiancée, twenty-six. Lt. Richey comes right into their hotel room at the Olympus, and wants to take them out naked. Wally says, 'All right, you can take me naked, but by God my girl is going to be dressed!' He started dressing her. Richey saps him. He was unconscious and naked as they dragged him into the station. His fiancée, equally naked, was right behind him. That's law enforcement, Tacoma style!"

On the way down the stairs I said, "Sorry you had to hear that."

"It's fine," Vic replied, "I need to hear stuff like that, and I know it's true, but Lt. Richey represents only about 25% of the Force, unfortunately, they are in positions of power. That will all change one of these days, if for no other reason then most of them are near retirement age. Right now, I've a sergeant that beats anything I've ever seen."

"Let me guess," I said, " his name's Tennant, and they call him Smithy."

"How'd you know?"

"Didn't want to say too much, but I had only to mention Moon, and he filled in the details of the entire incident. It seems one of Moon's helper's father was the president of the musician's union, and he called the police commissioner direct. Then Smithy's partner, Calahan, was called in and he finally concurred. Vic said, "I don't know what Calahan's future is worth, considering the code, but I'm certain he did us all a service. People say he'll be had, still I think he'll be okay as long as he stays in juvy; they're a little distant out there. That's probably why Smithy could develop into the freak, he is."

When we got back to his Oldsmobile, he asked, "Where to?"

"Ah, hell," I said, "How about your place?"

"You sure?" he asked, kissing me.

"It will be better than this Oldsmobile." It was.

Kid

I had a busy schedule that spring. Bob Summerise and I were promoting dances at the Bluenote, on my own I was developing series of jazz concerts for the Oddfellows Hall, and I was about to graduate from high school. I had a six-day a week obligation to Bennie's, and was rebuilding my pad. I was too busy, I told myself, for a serious relationship, but Moon was out of the hospital and doing better than anyone expected. I had almost promised Star, hadn't I? So at lunch that Saturday, I said, "I'm working the door tonight at the Bluenote, why don't you stop by with a couple of girlfriends? My treat."

"It's a date," she kissed me.

I'd always leave the store at six on dance nights, have supper and read the paper at Browne's, and be upstairs by seven-thirty, a half-hour before opening. When I arrived at the door Star was waiting, alone. "I told you I'd be here, and I didn't need any girlfriends. I just need you!"

"Well, let's go in," I said, taking her hand, "We've a little set-up work, then we can dance."

We cleaned the ticket booth, brought out new rolls of tickets, inked the door stamps, counted out $200 in small bills, set the screen in front of the door, turned on the jukebox, and we were done. Star was leaning over the jukebox, reading the selections. "This is your litmus test," I said. "Pick three selections." She picked Mr. B's "Everything I Have Is

Yours," Stan Kenton's "Artistry in Rhythm," and June Christy's "Make Love to Me."

"How'd I do?" she asked. I knew only Dela or Moon could have selected those for me, but said nothing as we slowly maneuvered the vast empty dance floor. She responded to my every whim. This was the first time I had had her in my arms. Her bra poked me in the chest, her pelvis flush against mine, her cheek on my chin, and her Shocking perfume wrapped all in an intoxicating package.

"I'm drunk, " I said.

"Me, too," she quivered. We sat out the Kenton number. It can be danced, but I decided to save that one for later.

"Now, tell me the source of your selections, Dela or Moon?" I questioned.

"Actually, neither, I'm not devious. I only know *of* Moon and Dela; I've never met either of them. But think of what's on that box. I bet you selected them, am I right?" I nodded. "See, see, I could have selected anything; so I went for the message rather then the music. They could have been sung by Margaret Whiting for all I cared! Actually, I could find only two that were appropriate, so I selected "Artistry" for my final choice because I love it and I knew you'd love it, too.

"This woman stays ahead of me, how will I ever catch her?"

"That will be easy," she answered.

I pulled her to the dance floor as the Christy number began, and whispered in her ear, "Now that I know everything you have is mine; let's see what June has to say?" We did a quick spin on the guitar opening and a deep dip, adding a soft kiss when Christy sang, "Make love to me, my darling." But, my body was starting to betray my senses; so we danced over to the entrance where I released her doing a cavalier curtsy. "You are the dance partner of my life," I said. She clapped her hands, did several little jumps, and gave a high pitched squeal. For all her overt sophistication, she retained some little girl mannerisms that charmed my depths.

My partner, Bob Summerise, relieved me at ten o'clock. Star and I held hands going down the stairs, stopping at the bottom for a deep, moist kiss. All I wanted to do was find a bed, instead I asked, "How about something to eat?"

"Not dinner, but perhaps a sandwich," she answered.

"Okay," I said, "what time do you need to be home?"

"Never," she purred.

"Wait a minute, I'm not going to get in trouble with your folks on our first night out."

"Don't worry my folks are wonderfully old; they go to bed at ten and are never heard from again 'til morning. They never know when I come in."

"Look," I said, "there's something I haven't had time to mention; tomorrow I have a date, and now it means *we* have a date, to go sailing on this gorgeous sailboat, the *Sanish*. And no matter what you say, I *am* concerned about your parents; if this is to be a lasting relationship, they are *my* parents now, too."

"All right." she said, "Just to be on the safe side, let's get a deli sandwich and take it home. We'll have the whole downstairs to ourselves, anyway.

Not wanting to meet friends, we walked up deserted Commerce Street towards Ben Dew's Deli on Ninth Street. Actually, Commerce is something of a misnomer. Although it has four lanes, it acts more as an alley to Broadway above and Pacific below. The hotels backdoored on Commerce, as did the town's two major music stores, and many others. Commerce was home to two large parking garages, a billiard parlor, several "B" grade restaurants, and about a dozen time worn taverns where old men stared into pale ale. Those aside, it provided low rent for a couple dozen mom and pop stores where you could get your hat blocked, your pants pegged, or your stamp and coin collections filled in. Below Fifteenth, many of the old storefronts, once deserted, had now become habitat for Gypsy families. Of course, where Commerce crossed the three major east-west thoroughfares—at Ninth, Eleventh, and Thirteenth there was a burst of activity. For instance, the Eleventh Street crossing offered a bank, Woolworth's Five & Dime, the unique Manning's Market and Cafeteria, and the city's largest men's store. As we passed the bank's elaborate window display, I caught our reflection, and swung Star around, facing our mirrored image, "Look at these pretty people, aren't they wonderful?"

"Yes, yes!" she exclaimed, breaking into her little girl skip, again. Suddenly she swung into me, pressing her body on mine, and turning those blue eyes on me, "And, we're going to stay that way, and tonight we're going to do something wonderful, and I'll be a woman at last, and forever your little hussy." Ben Dews' lit up the northeast corner of Ninth and Commerce, where Millie had moved after the Youth Center closed. She was now doing the late shift at the city's only midnight deli. Billie Holiday's "Lover Man" came from the jukebox. Millie, a master of non-verbal expression, looked Star over and nodded her approval.

She made a huge pastrami on Jewish rye; then instead of cutting it in half, she cut a third off, gesturing to Star and pointing her large knife at me. "Him, pig," she said. She scooped a half-pound of potato salad into a paper container, placed two kosher dills on top, winked, and waved us on our way.

When we arrived at Star's house, near Stewart Junior High, we noticed too many lights. "It's only 11:15, I can't be in trouble. Oops, I guess I was too excited, I forgot to call home after modeling."

She rushed in leaving me behind. I grabbed the sandwich bag, then hesitated a moment before tossing my long coat back into the car. I was met on the porch by a tall, blondish-gray haired man in his mid sixties, a short, dark haired woman, about ten years younger, and Star. Star was looking comfortable. "This is Curtis," she said to her father; "and to you, mamma, your *gendre*." I saw her eyebrows raise. I knew some private signals had been passed. She regarded me closely; then unexpectedly produced a warm smile, touching my sleeve.

"Wait, I know this young man. You're the one they call the Kid, " her father recalled. I froze, looking at Star for help.

"I'm happy you remembered, father. We saw him box at the spring smoker last year," Star piped in.

"Yes, yes, and you kept screaming for him after the fight was over, liked to take my ear off. Say, Kid, how come they matched you with that Negro boy, he was so big?"

"Halt! Stop! We are not going to talk fights. Tonight he's mine. Tomorrow, whoops, wait, tomorrow morning very early we are going sailing; so I'll be gone by the time you wake. She kissed her mom and ushered them off to bed, going upstairs with them. I sat on the davenport, awaiting her return. Finally she returned with two plates, two glasses, and a pitcher of lemonade. We were thirsty and quickly emptied our glasses. She filled two more. I sipped mine and joined her on the divan. We slid into its contours. Our tongues met in a bath of lemonade. I opened the first three buttons on her blouse, losing my face in her cleavage; then I rolled under her, slipping the catches on her bra and lifting her right breast to my lips, tracing her nipple with my tongue, and then opening wide in an attempt to devour it. We heard a slight noise from upstairs, she was instantly on her feet, listening. Nothing. She undid the remaining three buttons, frivolously tossed the blouse and bra over her shoulder, took my hand and led me into the bathroom. I locked the door behind us. She took a wash cloth and gently washed the lipstick from my face, and without rinsing, removed her make-up. A warm fresh face watched me caress her nipple, slip to her navel, then bringing her skirt and panties down with me as I caressed her perineum. My tongue gently probed the labia for the clitoris. She, at first, eased my head away, but as I gently pursued her, she relaxed, leaning her hips against the wash basin and clasping my head to her as she rhythmically rolled and lifted. At last, she stood there both trembling and purring.

"Do you feel like a woman?" I whispered.

"Almost," she said, as she again washed my face, she slipped my flannels down. I ripped off my dress shirt losing a button in the process. I put on a rubber, which she reached down and removed; I was powerless to stop her. My mouth met hers as my penis met her vagina. I felt, what I thought was the thin wall of her hymen tear away.

"I'm sorry," I said, "does it hurt?"

"Yes," she whispered, "it hurts so good." She was trembling, crying, kissing. I stopped. I could see a sizeable amount of blood on my penis.

"You, okay?" I asked.

"Yes, but I feeling a little weak, let's lie down on the rug. Guess I was a big talker until it came right down to it," she whimpered. We lay there feeling the heat of each other's bodies. I carefully kissed her eyelids, her nose. "I see those little freckles," I said. "I'm in love with those freckles." I gently caressed her lips, ran my finger around her left nipple, and watched it stand up.

"I'm back!" she said, rolling me on top of her, as I found her again. We began to move in step. It was like we were continuing our dance at the Bluenote, every silky pass in perfect rhythm. We were but two feathers caught in a liquid kind of harmony. It built to a breathtaking crescendo and then a crash of fulfillment. I felt for the top of my head, am I still whole? I questioned.

We lay there entwined for a long time, saying nothing. When at last I slipped out, I said, "How do you feel now, woman?"

"I feel wonderful. I feel like your woman; the woman I always wanted to be, "she said crying. We cuddled 'till she stopped. I reached over and took her hand as I had done months ago at Browne's. It seemed to me the promise had been kept.

I turned on the bath, picked her up, did a couple of slow dance turns, and kissed her. "Lordy," I laughed, "how can I stay an atheist when the gods send me something like this?" I lowered her into the tub, then went to the living room for the sandwich. She was looking comfy when I returned. You eat this, you'll need your strength for tomorrow. I kissed her again and did my best Elizabethan bow, saying, "Tomorrow at seven, bring a bathing suit, two pairs of socks, a pair of white soled tennis shoes, if you have them, and a very warm jacket. Lunch will be provided.

Kid

The next morning as were driving to the boat, I stopped on Stadium Way below my apartment. I pointed up at the Terry House, a rather small, 1920s building. "See that red brick structure with white trim?"

"I see it," she said.

"Now look at that smaller white addition, hanging out in front of it."

"Yes, I see it."

"That's the pad," I said. "It was added on during the war housing crunch, but it was run down; so I got it cheap and have spent the last six months rebuilding it. I love it, a million-dollar view! It will be our place, now. Don't tell any one about it. It will be safer that way. If you get a ride, just have them drop you at Ranko's Drug; it's only a block and a half away."

"Got you, Mr. Gumshoe," she laughed. "When do I get to see it?"

"On the way home if time allows," I answered.

The *Sanish* was ready to leave as we reached the dock. I helped Star aboard as Ken Iversen, the skipper, released the bow line. I held the stern while he took the wheel and drove her out of the slip. We raised first the main, then the jib as we sailed into a ten-knot northerly. The tide was beginning to flood as we headed towards Point Defiance. On a beam reach we left Colvos Passage to starboard, then turned more southerly as we neared the beginning of the Narrows. The knotmeter read five but we had about a knot of current with us; so we were going about six when we met the first of the turbulence just past the Point. Star's eyes widened as the stern moved sideways under the big whirlpools. Ken made her easy by saying simply, "This is what boats do in this kind of water." He was a lanky Norwegian who had a lot of blue water under his sails and moved easily around the deck. I explained that Star had never sailed before; so he took time to tell her what was happening. He also mentioned that the boat was a Lapworth 44, meaning it was 44 feet long and had been designed by naval architect, Bill Lapworth, with a turn of speed in mind but also as world cruiser. When he had the boat trimmed to his satisfaction, he turned the helm over to me and took Star below to show her around. The wind was picking and we were rushing along towards the Narrows Bridge. The current and minor whirlpools were teasing me and I was thrilled.

As we approached the bridge a Hawaiian woman about thirty appeared in the companionway, then came a five-year-old replica, following her, came Star carrying a younger sister. "I'm Linda," the woman said pulling her daughter to her lap. "The girls love to watch us go under the bridge."

"I don't blame them," I said, "I never tire of it, myself." The bridge was coming up fast. I steered towards the eastern abutment to give us a few more seconds under the massive span. The boat healed and the girls let out playful squeals.

"They always think we are going to hit the bridge," Linda paused, "and you know what? I do, too. The bridge is maybe 180 feet high and the mast is a mere sixty feet, but when I look up, I think, oh God, we're going to crash. But we never do; so it's always a thrill."

Star came to my side behind the wheel. "Let her steer!" Ken called out. I placed Star's hands under mine as the bridge slipped behind us. When I thought she had it, I removed my hands. We began to round up to port and I started to return, but she regained control and then did her squeal and little girl dance.

"Brilliant!" I screamed.

"Bravo!" said Ken.

"She's a natural!" Linda concurred.

We rounded Fox Island, leaving Toliva Shoal and McNeil Island to port, then beam reached to Smith Head, tacked to port and eased by Horse Head Bay close hauled, tacked to starboard well out into Carr Inlet, and then port tacked back to Cutts' Island. "This is my island." I said to Star, as we dropped the thirty-pound Danforth anchor.

Cutts Island is like a comet. Its head, the bulbous section, lies south, a sheer bluff that erosion has been chiseling away through the centuries. Its midsection is steeply banked with luxurious growth on top. North, it ends in a long tail, much longer than the bulk of the island. This tail at high tide, however, only show about 200 feet long, but at low water it's over a half mile. It's a magic piece of real estate, forested by tall Douglas firs, straight hemlocks, and twisted red madronas; its margins are richly shrubbed in thick salal and Oregon grape, and carpeted with luxurious grasses. It tapers abruptly at the tail–the spit, where seagulls chase rock crabs and devour huge horse clams, and we humans pursue Dungeness crabs and small butter clams. We lowered the lapstrake dinghy, and six of us squeezed aboard, hustling to enjoy the spit and dig as many clams as possible before it was reclaimed by the incoming tide.

As soon as we started digging, it was obvious that getting enough clams was going to be a simple task; so Star and I took the girls on our shoulders and walked to the end of the spit. At the very tip we were waist deep, and with the flood rapidly advancing and nearly a half-mile to walk, we are worried we'd be overtaken by the rushing water. But, like the bridge, you always make it; still the thrill is there all the same. The girls wanted to go out again; so we started out, but this time we only reached a quarter of the way before the tide and girls' screams forced our return. Star and I decided to walk to the top of the island and then swim back to the boat.

As we scrambled up the north embankment, we felt very alone watching the Iversens and the dinghy heading back to the *Sanish*. I guided Star up the central ridge to the place where the bluff breaks away into Carr Inlet ninety feet below. Huge chunks of rubble, some with trees still attached, strewed the beach. You knew only time held the chunk where you were standing, and the time could be now, but the view was choice–facing west you could see Glen Cove, south you could see Home Harbor and the cut between McNeil Island and the Great Peninsula. I took Star back a few yards to show her my den. The campsite was flanked by the twisted trunk of a red and orange madrona, which snaked through a bed of salal forming a natural seat. Moss and buttercups lined the four by eight bed in the foreground. Six tall stones lifted a small cooking grate out of the ashes. A kettle and a skillet hung on a scruffy alder tree. "It's charming!" she said diving into the moss. I lay beside her, placing several buttercups in her hair.

"I got an "A" in botany because of my flower arrangements. I think with what nature has given me here I could get an "A+". I picked another and placed it in her cleavage; still another found its way to her navel. "How am I doing teacher?"

"I think you're about a "B" so far; now let's see what you can do for an "A". I slipped off her halter and placed one upside down on each nipple.

"Now, that's an "A," she murmured; "let's see what you can do for your *plus*?" Slowly I started picking more buttercups, putting some distance between us, when I felt her arms grab me around the chest.

"You tease," she scolded, "I'm only human." Then I helped her hand reach my fly. I felt her face slide down my torso. "Are you going to tell me how to do this or just let me make a fool out of myself?"

It was a cold swim back to the *Sanish*, but the warm smell of steaming clams and garlic bread from the oven quickly revived us. Star prepared the salad fixings–tomatoes, green onions, avocados, and lettuce, while Linda mixed the dressing. Meanwhile, Ken showed me through the yacht's systems. Nothing had been spared to make it strong, fast, and self-contained–state-of-the-art was everywhere. The mast was a tapered aluminum section rather than the usual wood. The winches were custom top loading by a hip new company in California. Designer Lapworth's low drag hull made it the boat to beat in any racing circle. "This little ship is built to win at anything she does whether it's the Swiftsure Regatta or a trip around the Horn. That's what you can do when you throw enough money into a project!" Ken exclaimed. "But get this, Kid, this boat is barely three years old and the old man already wants to build another. He wants one of these new fiberglass hulls this time, the stuff the Navy and Boeing have been experimenting with. I don't know what he's thinking about, he hardly uses this one. He all ready has chosen a name–the *Shilshole*. It's another Indian word, meaning something like 'threading your way through a narrow, obscure passage.' I guess that's what he does in his other life. But, I do love this damn boat. I hate to see it go. Oh well, I should complain; it's job security; not that I'm worried, I've got the most loyal boss in the world, and he gets the best out of me for just that reason. That's his style: getting people to do exactly what he wants with seemingly no effort at all."

The lunch was something to dream about. When I dip a Puget Sound butter clam into wine sauce my senses start to go into ecstasy. The salad with the made from scratch, Polynesian dressing, the *burn your fingers* garlic bread, the chilled French wine–here was a feast of four worlds; all mine, and Star at my side!

The wind had swung to the south as we tacked out of the Inlet, Star got her little butt in the air and with long pulls, tailed the grinders while I cranked. We laid one tack into Still Harbor on McNeil Island, the federal penitentiary. It's a restricted area, totally against the rules, but fun. As we passed Day Island, the wind died; so we cranked the Perkins diesel. Star was at the chart table coloring with the two girls while I talked to Linda. She had met Ken at Honalei Bay in Kauai when he was returning from his second trip to the South Pacific. She loved her home in Tacoma but hoped to someday return to the Islands.

When we passed under the bridge the second time, the girls rushed out of the cabin and I took Star to the bow, pointing out the sights. "Over there to starboard," I gestured, "is Salmon Beach. See those small cabins? The only way down is that gray cliff behind, and you don't go there unless invited. It's the *baddest* place in town. Years ago it used to be something, now it's something else! I've been down there twice but only with someone who belonged there. There to port is Gig Harbor. It has a narrow entrance, kind of a dogleg, I guess you'd call it. That's what gives it great protection from winter's southerlies. I'll take you there in a flattie when we have time."

It was late by the time we had scrubbed the boat and got everything stowed; so we agreed Star would see the apartment next time.

When we arrive at Star's house, her father wanted to talk boxing. He couldn't understand why I had to box someone so much larger. I explained that when they had no match in your weight; they had to keep raising the bar 'til they had a match. In fact he had only weighed 151 to my 141; so on the card they added five pounds to my weight and subtracted five pounds from his. "Yes," he said, "and everyone could see the difference so they knew the card was a phoney!" I told him that when you fight at Lincoln you have to win to get your school letter; so what it comes down to is, you fight whoever they put in the ring against you.

Star's mom interceded; serving tea with a multi-layered chocolate cake. She was an articulate woman with a delightful French accent. She said William Gunderson had been an artillery officer; they had met in Arles during the First World War, they had a married daughter, and that Star had been a latecomer, "All the more welcome," she added. When I asked her about Arles and the impressionist painters, she got excited, mentioning that she had dined at the famous Cafe Terrace that Van Gogh had painted in Arles. I asked about Giverny, and she said her cousin lived in nearby Vernon, and that she had visited Giverny often. Obviously, she was pleased with my interest in her country and its art. I told her about my Anderson Print; so she offered to bring out her Monet collection when we had adequate time, but Star rushed out of the room and immediately returned with a very large paisley covered album. She flipped it open to Monet's *Field of Poppies,* "Mom's favorite," Star said, hurriedly turning to a woodsy portrait of Monet's two stepdaughters, "Mine," she pointed.

"This is unreal," I said, getting excited, "these are two of my favorites!" Star was on her feet, dancing. I wanted to grab her and swing, but I noticed her dad, looking left out. "You must have quite a different memory of France, Mr. Gunderson?"

"No, I tossed that stuff out with the war. I remember only Marie's France with its fine families, great Provence cooking, and the wonderful fields of lavender." Marie rose, putting her arms around her husband, and smiling lovingly at him.

Star grabbed me spun around and we hugged them both. Next, Marie broke away, kneeled before me, "You take good care of our precious daughter," she pleaded.

"I will, I will," I whispered, "I love her."

Kid

As I drove home, I was beset with guilt and doubt. I had found, or been found, by what to me was the most adorable creature on earth. On our first two dates, we had done things some married couples never find. What would William and Marie think of me if they knew? And then there were the enemies who could show up at any moment and destroy our romance. "Hey, you're the cat who stomped my little brother, I'm going to take your head off!" And, the enemy from within–Mr. Smug, Mr. Arrogance, who could blunder again and again as if on purpose. Then towering over all was the beast, Smithy–waiting, waiting!

That her parents had accepted me was granted, but I wanted to earn their acceptance, not by wit but by going the distance. Instead, I saw myself as skipping light-heartedly through a minefield with their precious daughter and my trusting soul companion on my arm. I fantasized leaving Tacoma. Ken has said he could find us a crew position with his friend Spike Africa on the *Gracie S* sailing south – man, the South Pacific, endless summer. Ah! A change in geography could solve a lot, except…except Star has another year in school, and parents she should never leave. I could leave alone, but then I'd be losing all!

I stopped at Moon's on the way. He was alone, sitting in the sawdust with his tenor, working on "September in the Rain." He put down his horn and passed me the fifth of MacNaughton's he was also working on. I took a swallow and passed it back. I explained my situation. He took another long pull on the bottle. "You don't have a problem. You can leave your present town, still have her and all the things you really want to keep. Leave the Tacoma you've been wallowing in. Get out! There's another Tacoma out there–the one in which all the square-johns, the johns we've been laughing at all these years, live. They go home after work, putter around the pad, watch TV, and then go to bed. They don't promote jazz concerts at the Oddfellows or dance bands at the Bluenote Ballroom. I know you can't get along without dancing, so take her dancing, but leave early; did you ever see a fight before intermission? Hell, no, the fighters come out when booze wins their minds, and that's usually near closing. The crazies are loaded; they haven't connected with a chick, and they are out to do damage. And, listen to me, there's another great advantage, you'll have more time for Star and the really fun stuff. Listen to me, now."

I did listen, and I knew Moon was right, but it would be hard to give up my Sunday jazz concerts. The planning had kept me going after Babs' death and Moon's troubles. If I were going to do it, this was the time because the final of the summer series was coming up. Moon had always wanted to do something at the concerts so perhaps he could emcee the final.

On most levels the concerts were working well. I had worked a deal with the union, thanks to Dick Morehead whose dad was president, that I only had to hire a core group at scale–piano, drums, bass, and vibes; after that anyone could sit in. We'd have beer and snacks for the guys in the green room so we made them pretty comfortable; then I had two cheerleaders from Lincoln blatantly pass the hat. They were costumed in see-through silks. While the musicians played stripper tunes they'd slink around holding a big top hat strategically; so as the customer dropped in donations, they'd attempt a peak at a little flesh. They were well enough covered that there was nothing to see, but hope springs eternal. It was great fun, and the dollars rolled in; so that some times the sit-ins made as much as the regulars.

We had a great pool of musicians, many came from the military, some still serving, but most discharged and just hanging around. A talent like Freddie Greenwell sat in on everyone. Part of the deal was I had to collect them before the concerts. I'd start at the Lincolnshire Hotel where Freddie and all his buddies stayed. They'd tell me where the others were; next thing we'd have two carloads. As I said, the system was working pretty well, we had great jazz, and great fans; unfortunately we also had great fights. Some even suggested that they were just showing off for me. I was the producer, emcee, and bouncer. The police were always threatening to shut me down. "If there is just one more call, one more fight!" they'd say. So when a tussle would start, I'd get a terror-driven rush, put two hands between the offending bodies and drive them apart.

One Sunday a good friend got in a fight with a sailor I hadn't seen around before. I was particularly enraged since the friend knew the problem. My rush drove them apart in such a spectacular fashions that the sailor was thrown over three rows of seats, all up hill. He just sat there, a little smile came to his lips, "How did you do that? That can't be done!" he said.

I turned to my friend ready to chew him, when he

put his arm around my shoulder, "Ah, Kid, we just wanted to see what you'd do!" Perhaps it was time to shut it down; I was there to support good jazz, not good fights.

So, for the final concert, I introduced Moon to the largest crowd ever. When he took the mike I could see he was having a good time. I stood in the back and watched him go through his Mooner routine and then pick up his sax and join Freddie in a duet. I wanted to stay and watch them work, but as the poet said, "I had promises to keep." I had said that to Star once, peering down her blouse, "Your boobs are lovely, dark and deep, but I have promises to keep and miles to go before I sleep." But now my promises were, indeed, to Star, and I intended to keep them.

I hurried to the apartment where Star had lunch on the table, a hot pastrami sandwich with creamy horseradish sauce and a huge Farman's kosher dill on the side. I put on a mellow Stan Getz side from Babs' collection. Star poured two shot glasses of Macaluso's red wine. We walked to the bay windows, a small tug was towing a double log raft to the eastern shore where about 100 others were moored. "Toast," I said, "To your parents for manufacturing you for me." We took a sip.

She lifted her glass high over her head, "To us! To us, and no one else, no parents, no friends, we need none, just you and me!" We took the rest of the wine in one breath. Then she kissed me deeply. I teasingly, pulled away, "Hey, our hot pastrami is getting cold."

She grabbed hold of my tie and pulled hard. "Listen," she said, "we can have moderation in all things– in our evenings out, in our drinking, holding up the shot glass; but there are some things!" She flipped my tie with me still attached over her shoulder and pulled me to the bedroom. Sometimes hot pastrami can be better cold, ever so much better.

Kid

The apartment proved to be a marvel. We never stopped playing with it and in it. It had a very large kitchen-living room combination, a small bedroom, a smaller bath and a tiny deck. A long low bar with six stools divided the galley from the living room. I had purchased an antique wicker divan and loveseat at the Goodwill. The new double boxspring and mattress rested on six cement blocks. One living room wall was partially covered with full-length shelving that held sixty-six books, 128 phonograph records, and a hi-fi with four speakers, and that was it. I wanted to add more items, but Star insisted that except for a planter and a coat rack, we let it stand–keep it sparse. That way, there was more room to dance and play. And play we did. The bath opened to both the bedroom and the kitchen with spring-loaded catches on the doors. The bedroom had no actual door, only a three foot wide vaulted and curtained opening into the kitchen; so you could play tag through the bath, bedroom, kitchen, and vault over the bar, dash around the other end, and back through the bath. The living room was twenty-six by fourteen; so you had plenty of room to dance, and you could get wild, too. You could take two swings on the deck, slide through the narrow bath, do two more turns in the bedroom, three turns around the bar, and then collapse back in the bedroom. Since there was no one above or below, you could crank the hi-fi to your will.

The deck was a wonder. It had two old air mattresses which we topped with a satin comforter. We'd lay there naked. She did track in the spring and drill team in the fall, so she was toned. She'd be all comfy reading Shakespeare for her Lit class. Lots of times I read Hamlet while she read Ophelia, but often I'd take my little finger, starting at her toe, trace up the inside of her leg and by the time I'd reach the kneecap her nipples would pop up; then I'd roll away and watch them subside. "You're too predictable," I'd tease. Then she'd try it on me; but most of the time she'd just be picking around my body. I'd worked out since I was twelve; for openers I'd do 100 pus-ups and sit-ups before breakfast every day, but she could care less about my biceps or my abs. She'd search around and find a mole and tell me it had eight cute little hairs. She loved my flaws. I had no facial freckles, but I had had a severe sunburn on the back of my neck which produced big ugly red freckles. They pleased her so; she'd count them, lose track, and start over again and again. I couldn't stop laughing, but she was dead serious. She gave me so much!

The first time Star and I had touched, I knew I'd never really loved Abby. But long before that I knew Moon and Babs had an indefinable awareness of each other that Abby and I couldn't fathom. But, now I understood. And strangely, I wanted to go back and rewrite the past and say, "Sure, I was in love with Abby," because I knew first loves never worked. I'd seen the principle in action, and I knew it to be as true as any of the social rules we live by. I was in terror of losing Star to a stupid rule. I knew something outside my experience could make me behave badly. In a moment of ignorance all my powers could collapse and what would be left was the rule, which says, "Your first love is just a loaner, you can't keep!" But social rules are not science; they are only what happens most of the time–I'd tell myself. Star can be my first love and it *can* last. She's special. I'm special. *We are special.*

I knew I still had some explaining about Abby. Way back, our first meeting, I was kind of flippant when Star had asked about Abby. I was certain Star wasn't satisfied with my explanation, how could she have been? On the other hand, I was certain Star was open with me. "I'm not devious," that's what she had said about herself, and that's all I'd ever witnessed. I was certain she had been a virgin, not that I cared, and not that an intact hymen is proof. I had read of a case where a woman had to have it removed to deliver her child. For me the past was past; what Star had or hadn't done was unimportant. But for her it could be different. It could be eating at her. After all, the four–Moon, Babs, Abby, and I had been notorious. She'd have to have unanswered questions. As these thoughts, this mess was rambling through my brain; Star looked up at me asking, "Who was your favorite girlfriend? I bet it was Abby, wasn't it?"

"Wow," I said, "and who are the others I get to pick from?" She listed three more. "Okay," I answered, "of them Abby was my favorite. Given the other three she was about a ten. But when I throw Star into the equation she's still a ten, and you are a thousand. Is that clear?"

"Yes, I know what you're saying, but..."

"What I'm saying," I interrupted, "is I love you and I've never been in love before. I had a great affection, a platonic love, to use your word, for three people–Abby, Moon, and Babs. We were a foursome. We played off one another.

Most of my feeling for Abby was my feeling for Moon and Babs–it was a unique family. But Babs was our little mama, the glue that held us together. I could feel her soul. I could. I needed that; I loved that; we all did. When her candle went out, it went dark for all of us. At first I wasn't even sure I could remain friends with Moon, but he was so wounded, so helpless. I had to take him back. And, after that I could see his soul, too." My throat swelled, and I had to stop. Star leaned over and kissed me.

"Now, this brings me to you," I continued. "The charm, the fantasy, the music, the dancing, the exhilaration I'd found in them was lost, but I've found it again, and more with you. You are my family. I need no other. And your soul, I don't just get a glimpse of it; it is here for me to touch and care for. I crave it! And, you can tease me all you want about telling your folks I loved you, before I told you; but that's when it was made clear to me. You were standing there hugging them. I could see all the love that had been poured into you. I could see your soul and I wanted to be a part of it forever!"

She slipped out of my arms and lay on the oak floor and cried. I tried to comfort her, but she continued. I put a blanket on her and cuddled, after awhile she went to sleep. I sat on the stool and watched over her. The next day we noticed a little salt ring her tears had left. "Like a *puppy pool,*" I said, and started to clean it.

She stopped my hand, "No, don't," she pleaded, "I want to be able to look at it sometimes when I think I'm really mad at you."

Moon

One Friday night, Kid brought his new chick to the coffeehouse. An electric shock went through me–*Babs*, it stopped me for a second, but only a second. It wasn't so much that she looked like Babs; it was that feisty little quick step, and a *Don't mess with me, I'm not afraid of you* attitude. I could see her at the tiller of a flattie driving the bow right into your midsection. Then, too, she had dark hair that wrapped around her face in a hip little pumpkin seed do. But that was all, the features, the shape were nothing alike. I envied him when they were close. I could see the adoration flowing between them. It took me back, I wanted to hug them both, I guess I did. I'm certain I wanted some of it to rub off on me. Dela, also, took to Star, you could see that; I don't think Dela ever liked Abby.

After that they'd come by every Saturday and help me open. Their schedule was Bennies and modeling, my place, and then the Bluenote. I'd have a sandwich with them and usually Dela would join us bringing a little wooded bucket of home brew with her. It was fine, a quiet interlude. Defenses were down and we could feel isolated from the world for a time.

Stella

Vic and I lapsed into that comfort zone that most couples hit after ten years. I guess those six unattended years just filled themselves in. I didn't have to pretend to be a little goodie two shoes; and he didn't have to protect a male ego. We'd dance at the Spanish Castle and occasionally at the Bluenote. Once a week, sometimes twice, we'd go to Moon's place. It gave me a high seeing him look so well and his horn sound so good. When Dela was there, we'd spend an hour just chewing. My little matchmaker heart tried everything to cement their relationship.

I hadn't seen Kid for awhile, and hadn't met Star; so I decided to crash their Saturday gathering. This was the first time since the Youth Center that the four of us had been together. Dela goo gooing Moon. And me... ah, will this crush never let go! But, Star was there to remind me of what could never be. I tried not to like her; I'd been successful with Abby, but Star's openness and obvious caring for Kid brought me to my senses. Dela, Star and I retired to the corner. It was endearing listening to her attempts to catch him. We cackled and howled. At the classroom door, or at the school dance, Star and her two girlfriends would set up a triangle, blocking his way. At the last moment the other girls would step aside, leaving only Star; and, the Kid almost running into her, would smile absentmindedly, and keep going. It was like Lil' Abner and Daisy Mae. She'd go to his boxing matches and sit behind his corner. He was such a big showoff. Between rounds he'd take a big swig of water, work it around in his mouth, take a huge breath, and blow the water up in the air where the lights would catch its plume. Star would hold her face in the air and let it fall on her, to her girlfriends' delight. Then Abby started picking him up after school in her sports car, her long blond hair blowing in wind and the whole school watching. Star was certain she was overmatched. When he quit coming to school dances, she felt she had no chance. Months went by, then he transferred to Stadium. Her mom sensed her depression, and sent her to their longtime family physician. She freely told him what was wrong, and then the old doc, who had delivered her, made one gutsy call.

"Star," he said, "next to your folks I guess I know you better than anyone in the world. You're as tough a little scrapper as comes along. Darn it, girl, I don't want to give you over to some damn psychiatrist. You go to him, look him right in the eye, and tell him exactly what you want!" He walked her to the street, "What time do you get out of school? You call me everyday the minute you get out of school 'til we get this thing worked out."

"And I did it, I did it!" she squealed. The three of us jumped up, squealing and dancing in the sawdust. The boys thought we'd lost our minds; so Dela and I picked up Star and dropped her in Kid's lap. Spilling off, we all fell on the floor, laughing. Dela, still laughing, crawled to the corner and began sketching. A few robust swings of her arm and Star's likeness began to take shape, then mine, then hers. This is the chicks' corner, Moon. Tomorrow, I'll do it in watercolors.

Kid

Bennie handed me a nice little chunk of cash as a special bonus; so we decided we'd redecorate. While we painted, we sent the cushions to be reupholstered. We selected a wild Hawaiian print. Star found a great buy on some burgundy velour and came home with a mountain of the stuff. She cut patterns and the upholsterer sewed us a bedspread, a valance, and a wall covering for the head of the bed. We thought it dashing, quite sexy, too. For the big planter box I'd built, we selected a miniature palm and two split leaf philodendrons. We toasted it with cognac in our little shot glasses. We continued celebrating by Shanghaiing Moon and Dela and bringing them up for a drink and hors d'oeuvres. They were the first to see the pad; so we were anxious to see what they would think. Star clicked on the hi-fi and Ezio Pinza's dramatic voice pumped out "Some Enchanted Evening" from *South Pacific*. Moon glanced around then settled into the Hawaiian print with a shot of MacNaughtons. Dela seemed particularly taken by everything, as she slowly looked it over. She took her cognac to the bay window and looked out; then she went into the bedroom and came out with a challenging look on her face. Star and I exchanged glances.

"Star, can I use your little boudoir in there?" she picked up her purse.

"You betcha!" Star laughed.

"Moon, are you the whore you always boast of?"

"You betcha!" he said, mimicking Star. Laughing, he jumped up, executing several whimsical grinds, then falling backward onto one of the bar stools, he spins sweeping the fifth, takes a deep swig and bows before her.

"Good, how much you worth tonight?"

"Fifty," Moon looking out the window at the moon drenched Commencement Bay, "Seeing there's all this romantic music, moonlight and everything. Fifty dollars and not a cent less."

"Good," she said bringing out three twenties from her bag, "Here's sixty and I want the works, in that sweet little red bed right in there," pointing. We three were laughing, she wasn't. She grabbed his sleeve and tugged hard, he followed. A minute later he returned.

"Moon," I shouted, still laughing, "you slut, get back in there. You're among friends!"

"It doesn't seem appropriate," his face reddening. He turned away.

"Wait, that damsel needs servicing! Wait, does this mean ... It does. It means you've been out of service since... Oh, damn, Moon. Damn!"

Dela came out of the bedroom, brushing back tears. "That's what a girl gets for having too much to drink. Come on Moonbeam, take me home." then to me, "Kid, if you ever want to get rid of this pad, I'm the one," she smiled, her loving way.

It never occurred to me that Moon and Dela were not conjugal, and if not Dela there was this other voluptuous animal–Vera. Since Babs she did everything but lay it on him, and Vera could test the Reverend Powers' will. Knowing Moon, I couldn't see how other considerations could be more pressing. After he was released from the hospital, we were all pleased when he immediately got to work on his coffee-house. It was more successful than anyone expected, and surprisingly, he was getting a light but reasonable living out of it. Next, he was back to work on his horn–perfect, I thought, he has his life back together! Now, this? Perhaps, I thought, that's why he's doing so well with his instrument–lots of sex, no sax–lots of sax, no sex! He certainly hadn't played much when he was with Babs. Maybe he was all right. I asked Bernie Sederic; he leaned forlornly on his bass, surprisingly producing this lovesick look for Dela, "Is that why I'm wait-ing in the wings?" he asked. We exchanged smacks in the shoulders and laughed it off, but I had to know the whole story. I went up to the big billiard parlor on Commerce in the off chance I'd find Whitey, I got lucky, he was practicing on the large snooker table. He and Moon were close in a dif-ferent way and Moon sometimes shared secrets with him, he wouldn't want me to know.

"Moon?" he said, "Absolutely nothing since Babs. I mean it. He'll be blowing his top one of these days. And, he's got Dela hanging on his tit. Man, I'd eat a yard of her shit just to see where it came from! She works for him for free for fuck's sake. That cat needs help, our help, Kid. Let's go to his joint and school him." He threw a dollar on the table, crammed his cue in its case, grabbed my hesitant sleeve and hustled me out the door.

Moon was alone behind the counter. He saw Whitey's face, "Oh, mother, what did I do now?"

Whitey went on the attack, "We've come for a blow job!" I buried my face. "You see we know when a guy gives up cunt, it can only mean he's turned to cock. And we, Kid and I, your best friends, who love you most, want to be first. Moon started to laugh, I was breaking up, but Whitey's stone face screamed, "I'm serious, here!"

"Whitey, you obnoxious son of a bitch, will you get out, just grab your hat and put some heels under it!" Moon returned.

Whitey threw a ten on the counter and sat down, "Two double espressos and drop the shit, you're talking to two paying customers here." Moon turned, pushed the preheat button on his machine, and turned back again.

"Look," he started, " you cats... Awe..." He turned back to his machine. We waited.

"You, look, Moon," I finally said, " we're just two, but I wish I had ten or twenty more of your friends here to hear the great Moon explain how he's gone almost a year without a woman."

"*Again,*" Whitey started singing in his biggest voice, "*this couldn't happen again. This is that once in a lifetime.*" He popped down on one knee, "*This is the thrill divine. Once more, this never happen before...*" He scrambled up and half over the counter, "You don't believe in this Doris Day happy horseshit do you, Moon? Life has only a few highs; the rest of the time you're ankle deep in shit. Come on reach for another high!" Moon turned his back again. "Ah, Stud, you were looking for love when you met Babs. Sure there will never be another Babs, but there will be a Vera or a Dela. Let it happen. For Babs' sake, let it happen, again!"

"That's right I do have feelings for Dela, it just doesn't include..."

"Perfect," Whitey interrupted, "you handle the rest and I'll do the *nasty* for you!"

I jumped in, "Moon, haven't you ever heard of recreational sex? It can start with fun and turn into love. It doesn't have to start with eternal love. Do it for fun, have the faith that the rest will follow. Get you to a woman, man, couple-up. Only then will you be complete. If you and Dela stood naked an earthworm could see she lacks the appendage and you lack the mound. It's the basic circumstance of all life. Couple-up. Alone it's too easy to stumble and fall. Awe, Moon, this has the odor of a tragic flaw!"

"Man, fuck your *tragic flaw*," Moon exploded, " And, fuck your soul-finding philosophy! You're a damn *soul finder*. Once you start preaching faith and soul, you're just another bible thumper. Get *you* down to the *Redemption Center* on lower Pacific Avenue. And while you're at it, find a soul in this!" He raised his index finger. "You know what's best for everyone, but it's only your idea of what's best. Let me find my own *best!*

Awe, look Kid, and you too Whitey, I appreciate what you're up to, and I'm heading the way you two boomers are pointing, but I'm on a slower beat. I don't want to leave anything good behind. There are things that if lost can never be found again. You can dig that?" He paused, looked us both in the eye. "Now dig this, both you cats: this lecture is over, finished, done. So, can I get a little peace out of your mouths?" Moon slapped the counter and turned back to his machine.

Whitey noticed the pictures in the girls' corner. "Hey, Kid, look at those chicks. Let's go fuck a couple of them!" I raced to Star's picture, kissed her lips and did a couple of grinds. Whitey did the same with Stella's picture. "Come on, Moon we've saved the best for you!"

Moon slammed the coffee on the bar. "Get over here you crazies, it's espresso time!"

Kid

For several months, I'd been bringing a brown bag to work. I'd take a late lunch and meet Star at Moon's to catch their practice. It was pure pleasure; Star and I would curl up in the corner, share our lunch and watch five musicians grow. Moon was standing tall; you could see the respect the other cats granted him. All kinds of people were showing up. Beverly and that little blond, Star's girlfriends, became regulars. Mostly, though, they were musicians like Traff Hubert and Jimmy Giles from the Pirates Cove; one was an arranger, Percy Smith, who always had new material for them to swing. He'd go crazy when he thought they had it right. So would we.

One day his shrink comes by, his tall lanky body in his ivy-league meatball suit, and gave Moon a pitch to go to Julliard. It killed me. Why didn't he understand? He was seeing the best of Moon, in fact, that's all he ever saw. Moon would go to his office and tell him exactly what he wanted to hear. And now he was listening to a talented musician, what could he think? I fought off the notion of having Whitey give the doc a call. I finally called Stella, she didn't seem to understand, either. Maybe Star did, that's all. Anyway, January 5th, I took Moon to Sea-Tac Airport for his flight to New York. In spite of my vicious harangue, he displayed the confident attitude of one who knew where he was going and just how to get there. I received a letter two weeks later, the school, the job, and the life were great. I was elated that I had been wrong.

Stella

The following week, Kid called me saying Moon was leaving for Julliard and New York. I could tell he was more than a little apprehensive. I did my best to allay his fears. I told him Moon's history was not Babs' and that Moon was a survivor.

"There's two things you don't know," he countered. "First, Moon used to sleep three, maybe four hours a night; now when he's not working, he's sleeping. Second, and more important he hasn't had sex since Babs. And, he has opportunities, ample opportunities. For Moon that's not surviving, that's walking death." Pissed, he hung up.

I called Moon, he wasn't home; so I called him at the coffeehouse; I could hear them jamming in the background. When Moon got the receiver, "Moon," I said, "I'm taking you to an early supper, when's practice over?"

"An hour, will that be cool?"

"I'll pick you up," I answered. I took him to don's. I wanted the full test. We sat in a back booth. The jukebox selection was a paged affair at each booth. I dropped in a quarter, "You pick the first two, Moon, then I'll pick the last one. Moon picked two instrumentals; then hiding my selection, I plugged "Once"–I knew it had been their theme song. His instrumentals played first. Rae, the waitress, came by. Moon introduced us as we ordered burgers and malts. Then I reached under the table putting my hand on his knee. He stiffened at first, but seeing my playful smile, he relaxed. "Moon," I said, "half the girls in town are *begging* for your favors, and I'm told you're turning them all down. You wouldn't turn me down, would you?"

"You haven't asked, yet," he laughed.

"Well, I am asking; I'm asking for all the healthy hussies that need a piece of your charm? The kid told me the last girl you slept with was Babs, what gives?"

"Damned Kid, tell him, tell City Hall, tell the **Tribune** - it's all one."

"Moon, this is serious. A healthy, experienced male goes almost a year without sex, with ample willing and attractive partners available–come on Moon; they have to make a special ward in the loony bin for a cat like that. I sat there and waited. He drank his water, swung sideways in his seat. A moment of terror came. He's going to bolt–get up and run! But then, he relaxed and shifted back into the corner of the booth. Slowly his eyes came my way.

"How answer you that, Moon?" he said at last. Rae plunked the burgers in front of us. "You see this burger, Stella? Well, Don's makes a damn fine burger. It's just something they do here, perhaps it's the sauce. I used to go to the Husk, Busches, and Lanes; but they can't touch this. So if I have a choice I come here. It was the same way with chicks. I tried a bunch. Then I met Babs–the sauce was there, Stella. I knew even before I tasted. It sizzled; it came into me; drew me out. I've got to find that again. I'm only half...I'm half... I've got to find..."

"But, Moon..." I stopped. Eckstine's voice silenced the room:

Once and only once the one and only comes along.

Once you took my hand, I felt your touch and I
    was strong.
The wonder of a simple love was not too clear to me,
Though you were dear to me, I walked away.
Who knew that once I knew your arms,
Your arms would bind me to the past.
I, who used to say, that nothing in this world would
    last.
We live but once, and now I know that my once was
    then.
Please take me back and love me just once again.
We live but once, and now I know that my once was
    then.
Please take me back and love me just once again.

Our eyes were moist. "Please. Moon, you can't have it back again. Most of us never have it once, not what you had! Rejoice that you two had this wonder to share. Let yourself slide a little. Open up to some of us lessors. Isn't it possible that this gift you were given you could give to someone else?"

"I'll try, Stella. And, if I can't; I'll put it into my music; isn't that how artists are born?"

"Yes, and you are my true artist, Moonbeam. Sorry for all my little tricks, but I had to know you'd be okay."

"What are friends for? The Kid will probably really work me over."

Moon

One night Kid and Star showed up at Stanley's. I was pleased because I was working it good that night, and I could tell the Kid was enjoying himself. We got a real nice response from the crowd at break, but Kid jumped up and called, "Move over Getz, here comes Moonbeam!" His approval meant a lot, one hell of a lot–more than it should have.

My C.P.S. class was only marginal, but the hardcore practice sessions at my place were paying off. Friends would come by and stay for the full session, sometimes a full house. One day my shrink came by. "Moon," he said, "You're wasting your time with me. Jazz is your therapy. Why don't I talk to your sponsor, perhaps we could get you to Julliard?" I chewed on that for a couple weeks, and then one day Star asked Kid who his favorite musician was? "If I had to pick only one," he said, "I would have to say Ben Webster. His voice comes to me, talks to me, whispers to me, comes into my body." I was blown away. I could have used those exact words. How could he? It scared me. Then I realized we'd spent four years listening to the same recordings, we knew all the same musicians, why wouldn't we think alike? Like Kid I had absorbed all the music I could, but it had all been funneled through Tacoma. Maybe New York was what I needed, and just when would the opportunity come again? I remembered the Kid saying when he was going to be a professional boxer; he would have to go to New York or New

Jersey. I gave the doctor the nod. Two weeks later I presented Dela the keys to the coffeehouse, and Kid picked me up in his cherry old Ford. I thought I was on my way to Sea-tac, but instead he drove me to the Bay Towers, pulled into the alley, and turned out the lights. We watched the lights come on in the '49 Buick as it slowly drove by. They still knew us.

"Moon, Moon …" he hesitated, " I don't want you to go. I know it's late to be saying this. Please stay; this could turn out to be another wonderful sanitarium in sunny Palarno."

"No, no, I need this. I have to grow!" I answered.

"Your people are here, Moon. There are five people I know personally that love you. I know twenty more that would carry your saxophone to your next gig and the one after that. That's respect, Brother. That's family. Few people get that much. Who do you have back there? No one, that's who!"

"I do, I do," I countered. "I've got the school, the tutor, the gig. And, my gig is with a small group in the village. That's family. And I'll have 52nd Street; that's every jazz nut's dream home! Tell me you wouldn't give your left nut to spend time there? Don't you see? I need this. Only in the City can I get the stuff I require to grow. Tacoma is dirt, New York is fertilizer. I need this to prove my music–to prove myself."

He put his hand on my shoulder in that familiar way, "No, Moon, you proved yourself to me the day I met you. I know that also goes for Star, Dela, Stella, and Whitey; and more importantly it went for Babs, too; and if that precious soul is still around, and I'm certain it is; it still goes for Babs."

"Shut up, you mystical atheist, and take me to the airport," I said. We drove the nineteen miles to Sea-Tac in silence.

Kid

For my birthday, January 22nd, Star and I were planning a new car. I liked my old Ford, but I'd seen a yellow and white convertible that had taken my fancy. It was still a Ford but only one-year-old. The posted price was $2295. I had $1800 in my cigar box, and Star wanted to kick in $200 she had saved from her modeling jobs, and with the three to four hundred I expected to get from my car, I figured we'd have just enough. That's when I started the chiseling game with the dealer. After two days I had him down to $1800. Once we could easily afford it, we didn't want it anymore; so we started shopping again. A new high roller outfit from Portland had just opened an Oldsmobile-Cadillac agency on the River Road in Puyallup. Their ads said. "Drive a little farther, save a little more!" Sounded like a good idea to us. Up front they had a group of featured cars with a large sign: *$100 off on these vehicles everyday until sold.* Star and I were caught by a black, 1951 Jaguar sedan. The price was $2895. She laughed nervously, opened the door, and peered at the gray rolled leather upholstery, mohair headliner, brier-looking dash, and sunroof. "Wow," we said in unison. I pushed Star into the driver's seat while I jumped in the back. "Oh, Miss Gunderson, to the paddock, please." She squealed her little girl squeal.

"Can we, please!" she pleaded.

"We must," I answered, "but it will take some doing–some strategy. When the salesman comes over, let him know you don't like it in no uncertain terms." I got out as a man in a dark raincoat approached. Star rolled down the window. I walked towards the next car.

"How do you like the Jaguar, little lady?"

"I don't think I like it at all. What's this funny stick between the seats?"

"That's the gear shift–four on the floor they call it. I must admit, it's a little different. We were asking $3600; now, it's down to $2895, a good buy.

I moved back around, "It is a strange looking beast, isn't it?"

"I've got to be honest," he said, "I think, as do all the other people here, that this is a queer one. If this were San Francisco, maybe; but right here in little old Puyallup–no chance. These berry farmers laugh at it. We'll never sell it. At 100 dollars a day, maybe after twenty-nine days we'll give it away. The boss took it on trade on a new Caddy, gave a bundle for it. Oh, well, it's his money. Now, what can I show you? What do you really want to see?"

"Ah," I said, "We're just a couple of dreamers, lucky just to keep the old pot we have," gesturing at the Ford.

"Thanks for coming by," he said, dropping us. When we got into our car we noted the date, make, year, license number and the exact wording of the sign.

"Now, we have only to wait ten days and the car is ours."

"How do we know they won't sell it?" Star asked.

"They may, but I have my doubts with that salesman's attitude. There will be some trickery if it's still here at that time because $1895 is way too cheap, but we'll see if we can manage it?" Ten days later we called, the car was still there. We went to the bank, purchased a cashier's check for the amount plus sales tax, and had a friend drop us off. We were going to buy our Jaguar. It was no longer parked with the group, our hearts were pumping, but we located it behind the body shop. Next we found our salesman and asked if the Jag was still for sale. He said it was, but we'd better act fast because it was headed for the auction the next morning. Star handed him our check, and said, "We'll take it!"

He stood there in disbelief, "The boss will never take an offer like this; that car blue books for well over three grand, and the Kelley book is still $500 higher."

"Were not making an offer," I said.

"Well, what gives?" he asked, looking at the check.

"Were simply accepting your price," Star said handing him a typed copy of the notes we had taken ten days earlier. After a snit-fit, a dash through a hoop, and two somersaults, we were driving our 1951 Jaguar MK VII home. The *Little Woman* was behind the wheel shifting the four on the floor. She pulled over in a scenic parking area along the Puyallup. The river current was bucking an incoming tide along with the wind, forming sizable white caps in the moonlight. "This calls for some celebrating," she exclaimed. I swung through the opening in the bucket seats.

"Take me, you hussy," I whispered. The back seat was spacious.

Kid

For my birthday, Star's mother fixed an elaborate French dinner with mussels and all manner of elegant things I had never sampled. After, we took them for a ride to Gig Harbor in the Jaguar. Star drove letting them know it was our car. On our way back, we stopped at the yacht club to see Mr. Arno's boat. Luckily, Ken was there and patiently showed the Gundersons around. Star showed them how she'd tailed the big sheet winches, they were impressed, and Ken exclaimed "Awe, she's a natural sailor!"

Leaving the docks, Marie said, "I want to see your apartment, Curtis."

I could think of no acceptable reason not to; so I said, "Okay, but from the outside; it's such a mess; you'll have to give me a little notice for the full tour."

Star pulled into the small drive, turning to her mom, "Nous voici arrive's" Marie stepped out, and walked directly to the door, waiting. We followed. I turned the key slowly. Star did a tiny shrug.

Marie entering went quickly to the window, "Wonderful view," she said. She studied it for a minute while I made Mr. Gunderson comfortable on the couch. Then she walked through the kitchen, regarding the open silver drawer, on her way to the bedroom. At least the bed is made, I thought. Then she swung into the bathroom where she was met by Star. We knew she'd be checking the toothbrushes. I hurried to the door. "I see, this is *our* apartment, too?" Marie asked.

Star took both her mom's hands, "Yes, Marie it is." She had never used her mother's given name. They hugged and started to cry.

I was digging for an exit line, "Is this a girl thing or can I join in?" Star pushed me out and closed the door.

Kid

Star's birthday was February 14, Valentine's Day. Dela and I had a party planned for her at the coffeehouse. Moon's group now headed by bassist, Bernie Sederic, was playing. Moon was scheduled to call at eight, after which Star and I were going to do my silly poem. We first had dinner at the Gunderson's, where I presented Star with an antique broach with a Giverny landscape on the face and our photo inside. It was a hit.

We arrived at Moon's at seven-fifteen to a full house–Stella, Vic, Whitey, Millie, Bennie from work, a half dozen of Star's girlfriends and many more. A large flat cake with Star's and my likeness occupied the center table. I was looking somber and Star was skipping lightly beside me, obviously Dela's work. Star had just finished cutting the cake when the phone rang. I saw Dela's soft smile go into the receiver, before she delivered the phone to Star. She pointed to the extension for me. When I picked it up Moon was talking, "When you asked me why Kid dropped Abby, I was at a loss, but I knew it made you anxious in that the same thing could happen to you. Getting away like this has helped me understand. You have to know that Kid rejected his family–just divorced them. Then when I left home we were both alone, we became brothers. Then when Babs showed up it was odd man out; so he took up with Abby. I had thought, like Babs and me, they were in love. What it was, in fact, was a fun circus–a fast exhilarating, tumbling ride. When Babs got off, we all got off. He and I went back to our brotherly ways, and since he didn't love Abby there was no further need. I suspected some of this the first time I saw the two of you together. Gone was the wild whimsy, the harsh competitiveness that had characterized Kid and Abby's relationship. In its stead was a mellow, attentive, and supportive attitude of a mature partner. There was also a glow that I'd experienced with Babs that I could see in the two of you. I was jealous, as Kid had once confessed he'd been jealous of Babs and me. End of sermon. Go kiss your valentine. Happy birthday! Now, please give the phone to Whitey.

"I love you. Moon," she cried.

As Star handed Whitey the phone, I strapped on a long, silver dagger with an absurd jeweled handle. I kicked off my suedes and jumped on the counter as the band did a drum roll.

"*Flower, flower!*" I recited in mock-heroics, as Star did a little shuffle dance.

"*I picked a little flower and pinned it in her hair.*" Star danced close, and I put it on top of her head. "*She didn't seem to mind, and I began to care.*" I'm really hamming it up, now. "*So I picked another flower and pinned it on her heart.*" Star dances even closer as I put it in her cleavage. She does a quick spin, leaving her back to me.

"*Then her smiles stopped! She casts my flower in the air.*" Star throws the flower high in the air and kicks it when it hits the sawdust. "*And now it's trodden on, and I have ceased to care. And I have ceased to care!*" I take my dagger out, hold it high in the air, then plunging it under my arm, and turning so all could see I had clearly faked it. Boos and cheers go out as Buz jumps on the counter, pushing me off!

Now, Buz has one hand high in the air and a fist over his heart and recites, *"Oh, cursed' love, what hast thou done? Thou comest on this blessed day. Though who's to say..."* But boos and hisses stop him, and Stella pulls him off, and then the band strikes, "Stella by Starlight." After which they do a medley of *moon* tunes, beginning with "Moon over Miami," then "Paper Moon," next "Moonlight in Vermont," and finishing with "Oh, You Crazy, Moon."

Dela opens the door, sprinkles dance wax on the sidewalk, where Star and I dance to an upbeat rendition of "Stardust," and then a soft, "My Funny Valentine."

Moon

I had sent an audition recording to my tutor, and he had found a trio–piano, bass and sax, that was losing its horn. After listening to my demo, I was hired without conditions. It was an elegant club, and I was instantly appreciated. I wrote, Kid, "I've found my home." My teacher knew more about a tenor sax than any man alive, and his list of graduates were the giants in the field.

"You have a wholesome sound, Moon; if you didn't, you wouldn't be here; so don't be shy. You belong! I'd describe you as West Coast cool with an acidic core. Man, that's a combination. For openers, though, I see some body problems; we'll be working on how your physiology relates to your horn. I don't want you to hurt yourself–wear yourself out before the first break. Then we'll be working on lyricism; that's your strong suit. But, I'm not looking for a young Ben Webster; I detect some of him in you, perhaps too much. What I am looking for is *Moon* with his brand new voice." I was impressed.

For my first lesson, he had me play anything I liked. He studied me with the intensity of an owl; then he went to the blackboard and delineated every minute infraction. This was pure mechanical stuff–what to do with your lip, the jaw muscle, your finger tip; then how to prepare your reed, your instrument, etc. After a week I was ready to run, but then I started to put his ideas into play at night and quickly found

I was getting through the evening with less pain. Next he presented a series of unlabeled demo records by former students that had made it. Our first session was devoted to listening for clichés. "You must have a repertoire of clichés." Next we looked for element of classicism, etc. "Look" he said, "There are just so many sounds you can bleed from a horn. Learn every one you can–borrow, plagiarize, I don't care. Collect the ingredients. They will become friends, part of your personal repertoire. From then on it will be how you take them apart and put them back together–how you scramble and unscramble that will create Moon's recipe. Of course, you're already unconsciously doing this, but not to the extent of a Charlie Parker or a Stan Getz. I want that for you, Moon."

Moon

Next, I went into a six-week rotation cycle; I'd trade places with a tenor from another group. And, my tutor would be in the audience nearly every night. My first rotation was with a tenor from an all Negro band. They called me "Token." "Token, you sit right up there and smile at the folks; we want them to know we's liberal. And, Token, don't you go sniffing around any of those little black bitches because you'll be rotating yourself back to the Village weighing 126 pounds. I was still playing catch-up when I was moved into a sophisticated swing group. It was a pleasant interlude, but no real learning experience, well, maybe? After that it was a big hard core dance band. I was second tenor. We had only one ten-minute break in a four-hour gig. "We can't let the sweat dry on these cats or they will leave, and the house pays us to keep them here!" It was a ruckus crowd, but if they quieted down for even a minute; we'd pick up our instruments and march through the crowd playing something fun and silly like "When the Saints Go Marching In." There was a great deal of hoke, but I was learning what it was to be a working musician. Still it was wonderful when I returned to my home gig at the Village. They welcomed me back. We all hugged, even the hat check girl came by and gave me a pat on the butt. A week later, I heard by the grapevine that the tenor I had replaced had, at least temporally, won his bout with the habit and wanted to come back. They were ready to say no to him if I'd commit, but I'd met him, and felt bad about taking his job because I knew his other chances were slim. So, I told them I wanted to go home for a couple of weeks and think things over. My teacher was disappointed, because he thought we'd made "remarkable progress."

I spent a couple of days hanging around 52nd Street, where I met Sonny Stitt, Charlie Parker, and Miles Davis among others. Did the haunts–Birdland, Hickory House, etc. I shot a game of Eight Ball with Red Rodney. My teacher called but I didn't want to talk. I wondered around the city a couple more days, then booked a flight to Sea-Tac.

When I arrived at La Guardia, I found the flight was to be delayed at least an hour. Since I was an hour early, it meant I had two hours to kill. I decided to walk the adjoining district. I knew a bit about it because I'd walked it twice before, but once was in the snow and the other was at night.

I asked a cabby directions to a good restaurant. The next thing I knew I was in the cab and the Italian driver was asking if I liked spaghetti? "My preference," I answered. He whisked me off to Mama's House of Dolls, a place I'd somehow missed on my earlier visits. There must have been a hundred dolls in the windows. I'd become a sucker for doll since Babs. My eyes searched the encased beauties looking for... And then I saw it, exactly like the miniature I'd burned with the phaeton only about a foot tall. I exploded. I ran inside and pulled the glass box from the display. An Italian woman at the cash register came at me. "Those dolls are not for sale, young man!"

"But I must have her!" I pleaded. She regarded me closely, reaching for the doll.

"I am sorry," she took the doll from my trembling

hands. "This is a special one for me. It was sent to me by a very nice man. She cuddled the doll, "There you are, you precious thing." she said as she gently rocked.

"But, why, why?" I asked.

"This is where she passed into her other world," pointing upstairs. "She had to see her mama. Now, I'm this one's mama." She paused looking me up and down, "Who are you, to this?"

"I was... I am her...Can I go up there?"

"Surely. There's a room clerk at the top of the stairs."

"What was her room number?"

"A-17, ask my daughter, she can help you." she called out as I bound up the stairs. A tall, dark haired girl was ensconced behind the desk reading from a large literature anthology, she peered at me over her glasses.

"A-17, available?" I asked.

"Sure, A-12 to 20 as usual. We have eleven steadies. Why do you want 17?"

Stella

After Moon left, I continued going to the coffeehouse
every Saturday at six; it was comfortable. The same people
were there–Bernie and the musicians Moon had practiced
with, plus Kid, Star, Dela. We'd talk about Moon, and Dela
would show off her remodeling. She had a talent for action,
especially in oils. Her art bristled with power. On one wall,
she had painted the American poets–Whitman, Sandburg,
Poe. It was hard to take your eyes off them, and they seemed
to be looking right at you too. On the other wall were the
jazz musicians–a chubby Parker, a moody Getz, a gaunt
Baker, all captivating figures. In our corner, she had refined
the watercolors; so the bouncing girls were more sprightly.
"Still growing." Dela said.

A heavy project at the U.W. forced me to drop out for
a month. The next time I stopped at the House of Moon, Dela
was behind the counter, a mini jam session was blasting, and
there was a full house. Dela nodded as I stood at the end of
the counter. She had one of Kid's cheerleaders from the jazz
concerts waiting tables.

"Looks like it's going well, Dela, I said. "Is it going to
be House of Dela?" She set an espresso in front of me.

"No, never. That's one thing that will never change.
It will always be Moon. I do love it so. I'll make it the best in
the world!" She reached under the counter, found a photo of
Moon's trio, a letter and two postcards and placed them in

front of me. I read them quickly; then read aloud where it said, "I sure do miss you, Dela!" Then added, "Sounds like he's doing fine, I'm not surprised." She told me Kid had a demo record Moon had sent him and that he was bringing it down Saturday, the usual time.

"Count me in," I said.

Stella

I was the last to arrive that night. It was uncomfortable as I could tell they had been waiting for me before starting. Confused, I watched Kid behind the counter; he had six shot glasses lined up, and he was removing a dozen more from a fresh carton. He had been drinking. He staggered slightly. In his right hand he held high a fifth of Mac-Naughtons. He lined-up the eighteen glasses with his left, filling each to the brim, spilling a little on each occasion. I tried to gain eye contact to get a read on him. I saw a frightened Star at the end of the counter.

"Toast! " he shouted. We all scrambled to pick up our glasses. "Here's to Dela, the soul of this house. Look at her! Wonderful!" He tipped his glass to her. "Look at this place!" tipping his glass first to the poets, and then the musicians. He took a sip, as we all did. Then he went over and kissed Dela, hard. Dela turned her back to the counter and cried. "I love you, Dela!" he said, then pause, looking down the counter at Star.

"Toast!" he screamed. "Moon, Moon, Moon, you magnificent son of a bitch!" We drank. "Here's his demo," he said, holding up two records. "Some of the best sax work ever heard! How about that cats?"

"Hear! Hear!" the musicians seconded.

"This is for you, Dela. He handed one of the demos to her. "And this one is for me! He brought it down hard on the counter, shattering it. "I'll never hear that sweet voice again! Moon is dead!" He rushed out, Star at his heels, she grabbed my sleeve as she passed.

"Help, us Stella!" she pleaded.

It took me a bit to get through the startled crowd, by the time I got outside, Kid was already in the car, Star looked at me begging, but the car was already moving, and she had to get her other foot in. When I got home, the phone was ringing, and Star was on the other end crying, "He won't have me, he's thrown me out. He won't talk!"

"I'll call him, Star."

"You can't. He's torn the phone from the wall, " she said.

"Where's his place, I'll go to him."

"Pick me up at Don's, I'll show you!" On the way to the apartment, she told me that after Mr. Arno called to tell him about Moon, Kid went crazy. "I couldn't help him, Stella. I should have been able to help him. Why couldn't I help him?"

"I think it's because you are the real reason he's losing it," I answered. She stayed in the car while I knocked on his door. He didn't answer, but I could see a light on, so I called to Kid, "It's me, Stella. If you don't open the door I'm going to break a window."

He came to the door wearing wet sweats, perspiration dripping from his nose. "I work out when I can't do anything else."

"I understand your loss, but why do this to Star?" I asked pointedly.

"I can't help her Stella. I can't take care of her!" he pleaded.

"You love her?" I asked.

"Yes, Stella, I love her. That's the point, I loved Babs, I loved Moon. Where are they, now? The people I love, die. I'm strong, I think I can take care of them, but they die. Babs and Moon were both dear, open, and vulnerable. I'd look at them and see into the core of their being. You see, don't you? Star is like that. Can I stand around and watch it happen to her, powerless to help?"

"Let me get this right. Is this *dear, open, vulnerability,* a flaw?" I asked.

"Well, kind of a good flaw, I have to say," he replied.

"And, you're attracted to these people with this good flaw because you can see they need your help. You try to help them, but in the end you can't, the flaw wins and they die. Is that it?"

"Well, not quite, but we could use that for a working scenario," he conceded.

"So now, all I have to do is prove to you that Star, while appearing to be this delicately flawed little elf, is really an ass kicking bitch that will be around seventy years from now watching you meet your grim reaper."

"Okay, prove it!" he demanded.

"Easy! First she spent two impossible years bringing you down, and hog tying you. When you were with Abby for nine months, it looked impossible, but she hung on. When you left Lincoln, she chased you down, and then she has the courage to go into Bennie's alone, all those men watching, and take you out of there. Now, that might not be what a man calls guts, but ask any woman. Moon explained to me your theory on dancing–if you can dance, you can fuck, if you can fuck, you can fight. How's she on the first two?"

The Kid looked up.

"I'll take that as affirmative. Well, now, look out for the last one; she'll come at you from every direction. Right now she's going to come at you from my car. You are going to give her a big hug, and say you are going to get together as soon as you get your head on straight. Don't make a permanent solution to a temporary problem. That's what a suicide does and you're not suicidal." He gave me a peck on the cheek. I pushed him away, "Yak, you stink!" I said, starting for the door.

"Hey," he said, you're not such a bad dancer, yourself." When I opened the door, Star blew by me. Clinging to the Kid, she ran her hands under his sweats and wiped it on their faces as they kissed. I shook my head, marveling at her statement. Driving her home, I lectured her on laying low, giving him space, recovering from the loss, and all that.

"I'll try, Stella," she said, "but I can't let him lose us. When he wasn't talking to me, listening to me–ignoring me; it was forever. He once told me that three minutes in the ring with someone fixed on hurting you was like three hours. Well, for me, these last three hours have been three years. But I found out I'm a fighter, too, and I'm going to get in that ring with him if I have to!" I looked at her, jaw set, her make-up running from Kid's sweat–stunning in her strength. I could see there was a match here and I shut-up.

The lights were still on when we arrived at Star's, so I went to meet her folks and explain about Moon. I wanted support from the home front. They were swell, I saw a trifle more into Kid and Star's relationship; the parents had a quiet kind of presence that could not be ignored. I could see how they could make the Kid feel an urgent sense of responsibility. They could make Kid feel he'd rather run than fail her–than fail them.

I also knew the wild card–Smithy–loomed larger, now. I knew Kid had wanted vengeance when Smithy put Moon in the hospital. What could he be thinking, now? Perhaps that Smithy had helped to put both Babs and Moon in their graves. What else could he think? What could anyone think?

Kid

Late fall I had run in to my old English teacher, Mrs. Herring. She stopped me to tell me her son, Billy, had kicked the habit–had thrown the horse. I felt so good for both her and Billy, I think I was skipping around like Star does. When she saw she had me, she gave me a pitch to sign-up for one of Dr. Ranson's classes at P.L.C. "He's my inspiration," she said.

I had wanted to take a literature class, but the professor wasn't giving any evening classes that term. Reluctantly, I signed with another teacher. He turned out to be a real twerp–a minister's son. Our first evening, he called a get acquainted session. P.L.C. was a Lutheran School; so you could expect the majority of the students to be Norwegians, Swedes, Danes, Germans, and in that order. Evening classes were different, however. Ours had three Orientals, several Italians, and at least two Jews that I knew for certain. Anyway, the professor went around the room inquiring of each of the Nordics what part of the old country they were rooted. He was working in alphabetical order. "Mr. Amundsen, Norwegian, isn't it? What part of Norway did your parents come from?"

"Bergan," he answered, then they'd pass some Norwegian trivia.

"Miss Andersen, I see that "sen" so that's Danish isn't it?"

"Yes, please," and with a very heavy accent she explained she was from a farming village near Copenhagen.

"Mr. Bergman, we've talked; so I know your family came from Stockholm."

"And, now, Mr. Dahl, often Dahl is a shortened 'Dahlguard' in which case, it's probably Norwegian. How about it, Mr. Dahl where did your father come from?"

"Gosh, professor, I really wouldn't know," I said, "he only stayed one night!" That got robust laughter from the non-Lutherans, but barely polite smiles from the Nordics. Though the classroom work was inane, I found some new authors to cherish. I picked, James Joyce's *A Portrait of the Artist as a Young Man* for my mid-term paper. I hadn't feasted on anyone like Joyce since Hemingway. I spent the best part of every evening studying. Star helped me with the final typing. When I handed it in, I got approval to do a like work on Joyce's *Ulysses*. It was a big book; so I went to work with a fervor. Star would usually join me at the library. We'd peek at each other over tall reference books.

After Mr. Arno called with the news of Moon's death I lost all understanding. I had too easily won all the battles, but lost the wars. I'd go from blind rage to incapacitation. Two out of three of the most important people in my world were dead. These were the ones I'd chosen to help–to protect. I felt like a pariah, whose every friend perishes when they come too close. I couldn't face Star; she was the third one. The one my sanity could never let me lose. When I was dying to see her, I'd scream to myself, "Keep her away; keep her safe!"

A few days after Moon's death, I received a letter. It must have been the last thing he did. I read it over and over, before making a copy for the coffeehouse:

> Dear Kid,
>
> I was looking for a title for the record I sent you, but none would come; then I thought, "Ballads for Babs." Ah, what else.
>
> I've never tried to explain my loss of Babs to anyone; perhaps, a bit to Stella and Dela, but that was just to hold them off. I could never get to the real issue because who could possibly understand? After you had connected with Star, I figured you could, but by then I couldn't talk to you either because you'd know the inevitable conclusion. Once I'd known Babs, there could be no others. I gave her all my love while she was here and I couldn't stop giving just because she was gone. Whitey understood. Only Whitey knew how desperate I was to be whole. And, dear, dear Dela I had nothing left to give her; to pretend would have been the cruelest thing I could have done. And, I find myself always looking for Babs. One part of my brain is certain she's still around. In Tacoma I'd go places we'd been, places I'd seen her, or even places we'd only talked about. I'd stand there waiting for her, truly expecting her to be the next person coming out of that doorway, around that corner, or getting out of that car. In New York it's been worse; there's so many little Italian chicks. I stopped one yesterday. The horror of enduring another fifty years without her is unthinkable!
>
> My music has been good to me, here. I finally found the voice I sought. I played my boomers to you and the boys and, of course, my ballads to Babs. I feel fulfilled, saturated. But music is music, and love is love. For me, just me, a life denied either, is no life at all. I have not lived my life in sor-

row, but ecstasy. I've had great love, great music and great friendship. In saying goodbye, I know I've been true to my love, true to my jazz, and I hope you'll add, true to my friends. As Babs said before me "I can't help myself."

Moon.

Kid

After the letter I was still out of control, I would say to myself, "There was little you could have done." Then the recrimination would come, "You lie! You lie!" I had to keep busy, trying not to think. Work was good, the library was better, and when that failed; I'd workout. I'd pound my body 'til it wouldn't work any more. Only then could I sleep.

Without Star, I had no distractions; so by mid term, I was well into *Ulysses*. That was when I stopped at the professor's office to pick up my earlier paper. As he handed it to me I noticed a "B" on the cover. I was hoping for an "A" but honestly I didn't know quite what to expect. A "B" I said to myself, for a first paper is okay. But, he said, "That was a brilliant paper, Mr. Dahl." I was almost to the door. I turned back.

"B" doesn't exactly stand for brilliancy," I snapped. He was behind a large desk, a tall stack of papers in front of him. He leaned back in his swivel chair looking uncomfortable.

"Well," he started, "there, there were, there were some parts of it I thought I might have read before."

"Why a "B" then? Why not an "F"? Listen, you never read a sentence of that paper unless you were looking over my shoulder!" I hammered.

"Well, well, if you're willing to swear that every word in that paper is yours; why, I'll change the grade to an "A."

He smiled, thinking he had found the perfect solution. I wanted to reach over and twist his skinny neck, but I pleaded with myself for cool. Then I thought I'll handle this as Moon would have, "Well, professor, this isn't the proper forum." I waited.

"It isn't?" he questioned.

"No, I'd like to swear in chapel tomorrow where we have a thousand witnesses." I moved over his desk, forcing his face back, steaming his steel rimmed spectacles, "I'll swear I'm not a thief and a cheat, and you'll swear you're not a cocksucker!"

I took the back of my hand and swept his desk, "You're fired!" I said and stormed out.

The next day I called Dr. Ranson, the department chair, explaining the occurrence. "I can't say I approve of the language, but the sentiment was surely correct," he said. "I'll be giving an evening class in American Lit next semester, I'd be pleased if you joined me."

Kid

I had arranged a meeting with Whitey at Jack's Pool Hall. I walked down the marble stairs to the first landing where my shoeshine stand was still in operation. I patted the owner on the shoulder. "Hi, Kid," he said. I stopped inside the door, still on the landing. Looking down, I could see Whitey, his Willie Mosconi cue stick in his left hand, staring down at the tile–beautiful Edwardian hexagon tile that had seen six years as a pool hall, five years as a penny arcade, seven years of vacancy, and before that twenty-seven glorious years as Tacoma's best brothel.

He didn't look up as I took the seat next to him. He was pushing the rubber stopper on his cuestick back and forth across the tile like an eraser. "I don't think I can read that letter, Kid. Give it to Don Smith and Joe Macaluso over there, you know them, they loved Moon. Don read the letter and passed it to Joe, who read it then dropped it on the table. Another picked it up, and it made the rounds. Don and Joe sat next to us. No one spoke. Whitey's cue made broader and broader strokes.

The letter returned to us in the hands of a person about thirty I didn't recognize. "This comes," he said, "of Moon not being a Christian."

"You simple, prick! You simple, prick! "Whitey screamed, "You silly sack of condensed cattle piss! For Moon, the Christian, it would have been too easy. He could have killed himself instantly; then he could have known he'd be with her forever. I mean fuck, sure he would have spent a little time cleansing his soul in purgatory. Shit, he did it for love, forgiveness is almost automatic. He knew his theology, he would have known that. It would have been too easy. Easy, indeed. But, no, Moon, the atheist, knew he was going to everlasting dust, oblivion, nada. And, he chose that, rather than live without her. That's class. I wish I had that class. Here, give me that fucking letter!" He lunged, catching the letter, quietly read it, and then passed it back to me. He then lifted his cue, driving it into the tile, shattering it. He sat motionless for a minute, followed by a violent shudder, then he whispered, "Is he whole now, Kid? Is he? Will any of us ever be again?" He knelt down retrieving remnants of his cue; I knelt beside him sweeping the tile with my hands. I handed him the large piece with Willie Mosconi's signature. He slapped it out of my hand, scrambling to his feet. I tried to rise; he put both hands on my shoulders and screamed, "Look Kid, get out! Get out of this town, this damn toilet, before you get flushed down with the rest of us! Forget Smithy. He's the inheritor, he gets this shit bucket. And what's that - nada, nada, nada. You grab Star and get. Work the details out later. Get!"

Stella

I called both Kid and Star, daily. And, I was right about Kid and Smithy. Kid said the commandment of the street was if someone messed with your friend he was also messing with you. He felt he was betraying Moon and his own honor by not acting. I knew he was not naturally a vengeful person; that had probably kept him from acting previously. I tried to find arguments, but how do you tell someone that vengeance belongs to God when they don't believe. What was worse, he wasn't talking to Star. I tried to bring the three of us together, but he wouldn't have it. When two weeks had elapsed I knew Star was getting desperate. Kid agreed to meet me at Don's; I don't think I told Star; something could have slipped; she has some clever ways–that one. At 8 p.m., Kid was sitting at the counter, second stool. I took the first.

He looked haggard, but put on a chipper smile for me. He was sipping a Pepsi. I ordered coffee. My thesis was going to be Babs and Moon had freely given up their lives, and they didn't require, expect or want him to give his life. I was working for an opening when Star popped through the door with Willie Hogan in tow. In what must have been a pico second, Kid's stool swung, his foot darted out, splitting them. He pointed at Willie, tilting his thumb; two gunslinger eyes held him. "Out!" he commanded, twisting his thumb towards the door. Willie started backwards, Kid was up, his hand in Willie's chest, keeping him off balance. The door flew open and they were out on the sidewalk.

I grabbed Star. "If you planned that smug little rich boy's death you couldn't have chosen a quicker way. Now get out there and see what your little crotch has crafted!" I pushed her towards the door. A large crowd had formed at the conference where Saint Helen's, Broadway, and Ninth Street meet; all traffic was stopped. I was at first, pushing Star through the mob, next she was pulling me, and finally we broke through. Willie was on all fours. His sleeve had been torn from his jacket, and was now over Kid's left forearm. He was using it as a vestment in a mock ritual.

"Now, after me." He commanded. "Our Father, who art in heaven," Willie repeated it. The Kid hollering like a drill sergeant, "Willie, I can't hear you!" Willie repeated, again. The Kid with his right hand, calling the crowd, "Willie, I can't hear you!" The crowd chanting in unison.

Then Willie screaming, "Our Father which are in heaven,"

"No, Willie, a *witch* is a thing apart. It's *who* Willie. I'm the priest here, and the words are 'Our Father who art in heaven,' Get it right this time, Willie!"

Then turning to the crowd again for a repeat, they chant, "Get it right this time, Willie!" Willie screams the line again, everyone laughs.

"Willie this is a solemn prayer and you're making a mockery of it, everyone is laughing at you. Willie, you've got to emote. What's our congregation to think? Willie, you've got to emote."

Calling on the crowd again, they chant, "Willie you've got to emote."

Willie starts sobbing, prostrating himself. "Ah, folks,

Willie can't pray," gently lifting his chin. "I always said, Willie doesn't have a prayer! Now!" he said calling on the crowd and they chant, "Willie doesn't have a prayer!" A wild cheer goes up, and the crowd starts to disperse.

"Come, hurry, Star let's get him while we have the chance." We each took an arm and guided him towards the sanctuary of the Beverly Theater.

Vic hustled up and took my other arm. "I watched it from the window in the Music Box. Pretty funny," he laughed. "You think you've got it under control, Stella?"

"You bet, " I answered.

"Well get him out of here, quick!" But just then Smithy's unmarked car did a U-turn right in front of us. "Oh, shit," Vic said, as Smithy bounded out.

"What's happening here, Marzano?" he demanded.

"Nothing much, just some tomfoolery. It's all under control, Sarge."

"Yeah, if it's under control what's that man doing down in that crosswalk?"

"That boy's unhurt, Sarge; he's just crying for his mother, " Vic countered.

"Well, get him up, get him in my car, interrogate him. Let's see who his fucking mother is? Meantime I'll take charge of the Kid, there. I got a call that he's involved."

I saw Vic's face distort as if to say, "What can I do?" He stepped into Smithy's car and drove to the intersection where he disappeared into the reassembling mob. Smithy turned to us, "You may go now; I'll be taking his statement. I won't need you." We stayed. I moved around where I could see Kid's face. Two steel blue eyes looked out through a brow of hatred. I trembled with apprehension.

"Officer, I saw the entire incident, I can give you a statement," I waded in.

"Lady," Smithy said impatiently, "I have a principal here. I don't need your statement; now, run along before I cite you for interfering with an officer in the line of duty." I stepped back slightly, pulling Star with me; but she broke loose and barged in. A second crowd was forming around us.

Star, now in Smithy's face, "I was with that boy on the street, and..." Smithy quickly put up his big paw driving her face back. The Kid's left fist flicked out, turning Smithy slightly, then the right went to the stomach. Smithy gasped, momentarily frozen; but Star bounded back and was between them. I grabbed her hair pulling her away, but it was too late. Kid had momentary hesitated. Smithy, sensing opportunity, lunged, getting a lock around Kid's chest; it had the look of finality as the bear hug was wrenching the life from Kid–his face red, then yellow, and then graying, but slowly, a moan, a screech, a twitch, a wiggle, and then a shimmy, and finally Smithy had only his buttock. That's when I saw that thumb from high above come down into Smithy's eye. Blood and mucus showered us. His hold crumbled and like a staggering bear he pawed the place the eye had been. The Kid stepped back, squared his shoulders, did a field goal kick on the animal's right shin; I heard the tibia explode.

Smithy, now down on one knee, the Kid screaming, "This is for Star!" catches him in the face with a right. And he was down. Star was in there first; I grabbed Kid's other arm; he wasn't coming, then Bernie, appearing from nowhere, got his long frame behind him and pushed, and then two more cats got low and we got him moving. A horse whisper came from Kid, "He needs more, I didn't get to give him one for Babs or Moon. He should have had one for them!" He was gasping and crying as we got to the Beverly.

I looked back, the crowd was scattering, but eight or ten cats were still stomping Smithy. It was like a dance; one would twirl and kick from the right while a mirror image did the same from the left. They had come to do their calling and only death would deter them. When the Kid looked all right I gave Star my keys. "Take my car, they won't know it. Get out of here!"

"Your car will be at Don Arno's," Kid's voice cracked.

Stella

I went to find Vic; it took some doing as his car was still tightly circled by the second mob, which I'm sure was oblivious to the real event. I started feeling giddy, singing, " The wicked beast is dead. The wicked beast is dead." They parted for the crazy lady. I peered in Vic's window; it looked like they were having an amiable chat. I knocked. Vic and Willie shook hands and Willie opened the passenger door and left. Vic slid over and I got in. He told me Willie had decided there was no incident, nothing happened.

"Of course, I told him we couldn't protect him, which we couldn't. Willie knew if he complained, it would certainly happen again, if not Kid, then some friend. No, it's best this way."

"The wicked beast is dead," I said. He looked at me for a long time in silence. He took the report he had started and tore it into tiny pieces, then opening the window he let the wind carry it away.

When it was gone, he said, "Let's go check." We walked to the body, a light rain was falling. Vic checked for a pulse, shook his head, "Looks like some gang took him out." He rose taking both my hands, looking me in the eye, "You were here Stella, what did you see?" A faint smile came to his lips.

"I saw some doggies, a whole convoy, probably a dozen cars," I said.

"Only a dozen?" he asked.

"Perhaps, more," I answered.

"Yeah, " Vic said, "this is that one we should have stopped. Looks like the Sarge died doing his duty. Must have been caught between the cats and the doggies. Probably tripped and got trampled to death. I've got to get a few statements." He stopped one of the cats I recognized from the Youth Center. "I understand there was a convoy of cars from Fort Lewis that started this?"

Bewildered, he stared at Vic in disbelief. His eyes came my way, then a smile of recognition, and then the words started flowing. "Absolutely," the young man answered, "had to be fourteen or fifteen cars, anyway."

"You think they killed that sergeant, over there?"

"To be sure," he continued, "he tried to stop them from beating up on the cats and they just stomped him into the street. I saw his eye go. A big, shitkicking cowboy jammed his old thumb right in there."

"If you don't mind I have to call this into the station, but if you can get some of these other people who also saw it, I can take your statements." Ten minutes later Vic was busy taking statements from a dozen *innocent* bystanders who all saw roughly the same thing. Another officer arrived and took similar accounts.

Stella

I decided to walk to Mr. Arno's. It was raining and it was two miles, mostly uphill; but that's Tacoma. I didn't need the exercise, but if questions came up later, you can trace buses and taxis, but not heels. There's an anonymity, anonymity and equanimity if you will, that comes with walking in the rain, especially the slow drizzling Tacoma rain. It says nothing is going to happen very fast; I'm anonymous because I'm covered with water as is everyone; so who's to notice? Calmness of mind and temper was good after the upheaval, and it was wonderful to see my Plymouth in Arno's alley; I knew the kids had made it! As I approached a pair of headlights showed; then Mr. Arno came out, inviting me to coffee. The same male served us from the silver cart.

"I know I can trust you, but I don't want you to have information someone could force from you by some shenanigans. Any of us could be questioned on these late events. So please don't tell me anything, either. And I think we both agree you were never here." He paused. "I do want to assure you though that the kids are nicely tucked away."

"Kids, did they go together?" I asked.

"Indeed, I could never be responsible for separating couples again. Now, what I don't know is how to deal with the parents; I'm hoping you can help me with that."

"The only option, I believe, is to tell them what is essentially the truth: that the kids ran away together."

"Yes, yes," he said, almost animated for the first time, "Isn't it wonderful? I sometimes wake rejoicing. Babs and Moon ran away together. They're alive and living in California. Running away is wonderful. But, but… I'm afraid Star's parents wouldn't see it that way, certainly not at this stage."

"No, they won't; they will think the worst, that she was taken against her will, that she's pregnant, that Lucifer has taken control of her senses or any one of a hundred other horrors. What they will need is letters of reassurance from both of them, and immediately."

"Good," he said," I had not thought of that; it can be arranged. I have already asked a priest, who has met Kid and, of course, the Reverend Powers, now in Seattle, to write letters of character. Yes, and with letters from the kids themselves that should alleviate the worst of their fears."

On parting we agreed to have lunch in thirty days to exchange the hidden details.

Stella

A week went by and things began to cool. The *Tribune* ran stories about cats rioting with soldiers, but largely the soldiers had taken the blame; in fact several stories had been written about the "heinous eye-killing cowboy." Finally, saner articles began to appear, calling it youth riots and asking that youth centers and USOs be re-established. It was noted that no riots had occurred when the Youth Center was in operation.

I was dying for some word from the kids, but nothing! I called Star's parents; they mentioned the letters, but I knew that source. I was pleased they were taking it better than expected. In spite of it all they expressed confidence in both kids. I liked those people.

I started going to the House of Moon daily, thinking some news would await me, but Dela always just shook her head. On the plus side Dela was about the only one in town I really wanted to talk with, our favorite people had been removed from us, so we shared a vice-like bond. I've always envied artists, in times of trouble their craft can thrive, and Dela's overwhelmed me. There had been a muslin sheet over the back wall. One day it was gone, and there stood Moon and Babs in a life-sized oil–so lifelike, they were caught in mid-step the way a stop action camera might have. But, only Dela's camera could do this–they were both looking straight ahead; no question they knew exactly where they were going. I stood there and foolishly cried. Finally, I went back and touched Babs' arm, I had to.

Dela put her arm around me. "I could not have done that a few months ago," she said. "I've been told they're uncanny in their likeness; that's what I wanted, but more I want there to be nothing ethereal about them, down to earth where they lived, coming right at you, saying were in love, let the world know! I know it's part of my cleansing. I had to do it, no choice. I hated her for so long, but after Moon died. Well, I've strangely come to love her, too. I was his, but he was never mine. He was always hers, Stella; I know that, now. After I started painting, I could see it. I could feel it. They belong together, forever.

I went back to the *chicks' corner* to look at the three bouncing girls, they were looking a little pale in watercolors next to the oils, but I was still proud. "Looks like you've everyone here but the Kid." I said.

"You wait, I have something planned; you'll see one of these days."

By the end of the third week, articles were coming out titled, "What we learned from the riot?"

Nothing remotely connected to the Kid had appeared, and Vic said there was nothing at the station. "The unspoken sentiment among the Force was if we have to lose one of our own, Smithy was the best choice." Obviously no one connected the Kid with Smithy's death. I called Star's parents several times and several days in succession. No answer; something was up. I had to know. I called Mr. Arno, he agreed it was time to talk, offering to take me to dinner at Crawford's Seafoods, the best restaurant in town.

Stella

A conservative gray Cadillac sedan pulled into my drive, and a smartly uniformed chauffeur escorted me to the car. Mr. Arno spoke first, "I had Moon's remains interned next to Babs' at Mountain View Cemetery."

"Wonderful," I sighed, then I know there's something you'll want to see." I asked the driver to stop at the House of Moon on the way. Mr. Arno went immediately to Babs' portrait.

Turning to Dela, "Do you mind if I touch?" I could see his eyes were moist. We didn't talk the short distance to the restaurant. At Crawford's Mr. Arno gave me the seat with the view, taking the Hickok seat in the corner for himself. The waiter took our wine and appetizer order. Mr. Arno began, "When I saw you last, the kids were aboard the *Sanish* with Ken Iversen at the helm on their way to Port Townsend to provision. But April isn't the best time for West Coast passagemaking; so they had a spirited voyage to San Francisco, Sausalito actually. Still, they got their sea legs and now they're set. Then last Thursday the *Sanish* with Star's parents, her sister, and her two girlfriends aboard sailed under the Golden Gate, where another passenger, the Reverend Powers, pronounced them man and wife." I squealed with joy, interrupting him and bringing some unwanted notice. He put his hand on mine helping me settle down. "From here on," he continued, "It's points south–Mexico, Hawaii,

French Polynesia, and who knows where? A cruise I've always wanted to make. It is pleasing they will be doing in my former boat."

"But the boat?" I asked.

"Ah yes, the boat, the *Sanish*. I'm already building the *Shilshole*. I've given them the old one; it seemed the least I could do; besides when I finish with an asset like the phaeton or *Sanish,* their continued presence becomes a nuisance to be eliminated. The kids will have some funds and certainly time enough to put the little ship through its paces. I do envy them, though–to be free to sail where you please. Ah, such..."

"Wait, wait!" I interrupted, "Who are you kidding, are you trying out for sainthood? You have Moon's body delivered from New York and buried with your daughter. You give Kid a yacht worth tens of thousands. These are generous acts."

"Not generosity, it's called restitution. I've made so many costly mistakes, costly to others! Of course with Moon, I could never begin to..." a tear started down his cheek, he brushed it off. "But with the Kid," he rallied, "he did me a colossal service!"

"How so?"

"He dispatched the beast, Smithington Tennant." Again, assuming his inscrutable pose, the words came out one by one. "Something I've wanted done since 1946, you can't know. It was my goal, my mission, my dream. But something I could never do because it was expected. They were making book on it."

"But you could never have known the Kid would..."

"Ah, but I did," animated now, "not when, where, or

how; still I knew once the right elements were in place, he would act. You see I first saw the Kid as a callow thirteen-year-old street kid. He walked into my gym, all the confidence, ability, and will imaginable. My man, Bianco went crazy for him. He was going to send him to New Jersey when he was barely sixteen. We'd have made a champion of him, but the trainer, Harry Anderson, had a change of heart. You see, he'd watched the Kid since he was seven. Imagine that? He said even a winner in boxing turns out a loser. I knew that to be true, but that was our business; so I ignored Harry for awhile. Then I thought of another use for him. I thought of Smithy. The Kid, by the way, I'm the one who gave him that moniker, all I had to do was put it on the fight card and it stuck. Anyway, the Kid had to lose a fight to get him out. I called a favor with Ernie Jensen, the ref, and that was it–the Kid beats the guy silly and loses by two points, almost comical, don't you think?"

"But how could you predict? No one could!"

"I have seen six of his matches. You have seen him fight, at least once. He always does what it takes to win, just that, no more. Bianco says he puts just the right wiggle to take him over the top. That's the first thing we need to know. Then he has that righteous bent to his character. That's the second thing. He must do right by his people–he must help them, save them, avenge them. He can do no other. My plan was to bring him in contact with Babs, but I didn't have to; Moon accomplished that for me. He felt for her the way I knew he would. He saw in her some sense of art and grace he felt lacking in himself. He was the perfect instrument. Unfortunately, Babs' death was so clouded. He knew Smithy was the prime mover in Babs' mental breakdown, but there were too many others with partial blame–the doctor, me, even Moon and Abby, in the Kid's mind. How could he act?

The second opportunity was Moon's beating and subsequent hospitalization. Had it happened then he would have been the only suspect–disaster! So I made some moves to prevent it. They worked rather well, don't you think? But with Moon's death, the third fall, I knew there would be no stopping him; so I called him in and provided several escape routes. You and Vic provided the rest of the help he needed, for which I will be eternally grateful. I can see Vic with Sergeant's stripes before long." He paused, I wanted to say something, "Thank you," anything; but my mind was too busy trying to unravel what it had just taken been given. I pulled the olive around my martini by its stem and stared into its amber liquid. I couldn't look at him.

Thankfully, he continued, "Oh, by the way, the Kid sent two sets of keys he won't be needing. This set is for Dela; it's the apartment. The Kid says she will enjoy it. The second set is for you, it's the Jaguar. I've seen your Plymouth, I know you will enjoy it!"

After my second drink, I said, "They were the two greatest young men I'd ever known or hope to know."

"Yes," he said, not just young men, but *men*. They had love, courage, and loyalty in massive doses. I took them into my family–my son and my son in law. So you see, it wasn't charity to bury Moon next to Babs, he belonged!"

"Well," I said, "they are safe, now."

"So they are, one permanently and one, at least temporary; but I've lost them both, I've lost them all. He turned his body to look out the window: it was an awkward stretch. I couldn't see if he was crying because I was.

Stella

In spite of his grisly business that made him the richest and most powerful man in the Northwest, he was one of the most appealing human beings I had ever met. And still, he was an enigma. He loved the Kid as a son, yet he would use him as a tool to avenge his daughter's destruction. I have sometimes thought of myself as a social engineer. I engineer the induction of young people into the system, by getting them to accept, then follow both the written and unwritten rules of society. This indoctrination is sometimes, hell often, accomplished by devious means. But, if what Mr. Arno said was true, next to him I am still just playing with erector sets. He thinks he engineered a right-eous young man, a social worker, and a policeman to commit a perfect murder. But had he? I had to pat myself on the back; I had told him almost nothing, and let him get everything off his chest–standard social work. Specifically, I hadn't told him that Kid didn't kill Smithy. He was breathing loud and clear when we pulled Kid away. And, I didn't tell him the Kid's act was not vengeance. Kid had not been present to protect Moon or Babs, so he felt he had not done his duty. But he was there to protect Star, and he had done his sacred duty. He would be able to live with that, rather nicely, I think. You'd have to say what the cats did: the execution, was pure vengeance, but that was theirs not Kid's. But why mess with illusions; Mr. Arno had his and some good people had benefited; and for once the right person had died and the streets will be better for it.

It was several days before I could get to Dela with the apartment keys, and when I did I was driving the Jaguar. Bernie saw the car being parked and came running out; thinking it was the Kid. "It's only me I said." I said, seeing his disappointment. He put his arm around me, escorting me inside. Dela came from behind the muslin curtain, now covering the corner. I was heartsick–the bouncing girls gone? I loved those girls and had deep pride in being one of them. "You didn't?" I asked, Dela.

"Darling, Stella, you come by Saturday for the dedication; I promise you won't be disappointed."

I told her the developments with Kid and Star, which brought tears to her eyes. Bernie put his arm around her waist, giving her a soft kiss. You could see they were a couple. It pleased me so.

"Oh, I almost forgot, Kid sent these keys, the apartment is yours now!"

She did a little Star skip and squeal as we walked towards the car. Then she turned to Bernie, "Come on, Stud, I've got a little burgundy boudoir to show you." They locked the door and skipped off toward their new apartment.

Stella

Saturday evening, Vic and I took the table in the center of the room. Bernie with his quartet was playing Moon's "Ballads for Babs." The muslin curtain still hid the surprise. Dela was working behind the counter and two cheerleaders were now serving. Vic inspected the new deli menu, "Boy, this place is getting a little pricey!"

"Go on," I said, "I love it when you talk cheap to me." He kicked me under the table, "Look," I continued, "how this place has been upscaled since I first brought you here."

The group then played a soft rendition of "Once." Dela stood by the portrait and we all toasted Moon and Babs. After a moment of silence, Dela and Bernie, one on either side removed the curtain to a soft drum roll. A sigh went up from the house. The three girls were there as before, but now they were full sized and in oils. But holding Star's hand as if to bring her back down to earth was Kid. A joyous audience applauded vigorously. We toasted Kid and Star. Then another drum roll. I turned back to Vic and he was on his knees. "Stella by Starlight" was softly spoken by the saxophone as Vic placed a diamond in a tiffany setting on my finger.

"Ah shit, a little fluff will turn me to goo!"

Epilogue

It continued as a dream in soft sunshine. And so, the soft westerly lifted the spinnaker and then watched as it collapsed, allowing the *Sanish* only slow progress down the Strait of Juan de Fuca, but at Admiralty Inlet the northerly filled the Haida hawk designed into the sail, spread its wings and soared. A dark haired woman guided the helm with a steady hand. A small blond boy at play clutched her right leg, swinging with the rhythm of the sea.

"Is this the Puget Sound, Mama?" he asked.

"Yes, Raymond, that's Point Wilson over there. See it?"

"I see it," he replied, "but what's that?" pointing to the other shore.

"That's Admiralty Head," she answered.

"Does it got a head?"

"Not exactly," came the eager male voice from the companionway, "but it sticks up above the rest so that's what they call it." He joined them at the wheel throwing a blanket over their shoulders, then enthusiastically engulfing them in his arms.

"Will anyone still know us, Star?" he asked.

"You bet they'll still know the old Kid, but I'll just have to introduce them to my Curtis."

"That's my woman," he laughed, "but will anyone want to know an old square-john like that?"

"Ah sure," she said, her free hand reaching for his face. "They'll want to know a world class sailor, circumnavigator, loving husband and father. You'll always have your fans! Little Bill will be waiting there to see you, but he won't have Miss Marie with him because we know first loves never work; except for us because *we're special*," she kissed him, laughing. "Now, name the first three you'd like to see."

"The ones I can't," he paused, "Mary Lee, Babs, and Moon."

A tear rolled down Star's cheek, "I know, I know."

Marrowstone Island slid by to starboard, then Whidbey to port. Next, they slipped through the fishing fleet at Point No Point, the tanks at Edmonds appeared to port, followed by the new marina being constructed at Shilshole Bay.

The stiff breeze meeting the opposing tide at Elliott Bay bred an angry sea, and the spinnaker came down behind the main as the *Sanish* continued under the main alone.

They shot the gap at Point Southworth into Colvos Passage, jibed at Fern Cove, and ten miles later Point Defiance loomed to starboard as the *Sanish* reached across Dalco Passage to the Tacoma Yacht Club. The slag breakwater showed bronze in the evening sun as the main came down.

Order form:

Title: Streets of Tacoma
U.S. Price: $15.00
Can. Price: $21.00
Shipping: Add $5.00 for shipping
Sales tax: (WA State residents only) add 8.6%

Send cash, checks, or money orders to:

Marjorie Hanson
1047 S. Jackson Av.
Tacoma, Wa.98465
Be sure to enclose your return address.